I Can't Go On Without You

A Novella

Serica Rena'

Where It All Began....

Brittysh

"I'm over this shit!"

"Oh, stop complainin' so damn much. It's not that serious."

"Yes, the hell it is! Why the hell do you always want to go out *every* damn Friday night? There has to be something else to do besides that shit."

"Please tell me something else we can do on a Friday night around here. Before you even open your mouth, I'll answer that for you. There ain't shit else to do."

"Obviously, you have all the answers, so I'm not going to even waste my time trying to answer that question for your ass anyway. What you need to do is get a damn hobby or something because this shit is getting old."

"Whatever! You're just boring as hell. Besides, we're just doing what young bitches like us are supposed to do after workin' all damn week. We need to get out of the house and have some damn fun at least one night out of the week, sis."

"Girl, I hear you, but I'm not feelin' this shit tonight. I'm sleepy as hell, Karmyn. I had a busy ass week, and today was even worse."

"You act like an old-ass lady. Bitch, you ain't but 24 years old."

"I don't *act* like an old lady."

"Yes, the hell you do, but I know exactly what you need to change that shit."

"I bet you do, and I'm sure you're about to tell me too."

"Hell yeah! If I don't let yo' ass know, who will? It definitely won't be yo' momma."

"Whatever! Don't even go there."

"I won't, but you know I'm right. Anyway...."

"Karmyn, just tell me whatever it is you're trying to tell me, so you can get out of my face. I already told you I'm not in the mood to deal with you tonight."

"You so damn grouchy just like *Oscar*."

"Who the *hell* is *Oscar*? You better not be talking about that damn character from *Sesame Street* that was in the trash can."

"See, you already know who he is because you act just like him. He might be related to yo' ass. Shit, he has to be because yo' momma is just as bad as you are. She always complainin' about some shit too."

"Shut up, Karmyn! You are really getting on my last damn nerves."

"You wouldn't have that problem if you just listen to me. Girl, all you need is a lil' dick in ya life to get you right. Shit, I know that damn fake ass dick you got hidden in that damn pillowcase tired of yo' ass by now."

"What?"

"Are you *seriously* trying to pretend like you don't know what I'm talking about?"

"I don't! What are you talking about?"

"Don't even try it. I found your little hiding spot months ago, but I decided not to expose your ass. I knew you would try to deny that shit. No need to hide it, sis. I see why you are satisfied with that big ol' thang, though. It's huge."

"Just shut up, Karmyn, and stop going through my shit. You get on my nerves when you do shit like that. What were you doing in my bedroom anyway?"

"I was trying to *sleep* until I somehow accidentally turned your little secret on. Girl, I couldn't figure out where all that noise was coming from. My head was already throbbing from all that damn liquor I had drunk the night before, and that shit just made it hurt worse. When I finally found it, I almost passed out when I saw that shit. I couldn't believe you had something like that and never told me about it. That shit big as hell."

"Tell you for what? You don't have to know everything about me, especially something like that, and it's not *that* big."

"Shit! Girl, that's some serious **dick dick** you got in that damn pillowcase. If that ain't shit to you, all I can say is *damn*."

"Kamryn! I don't want to have this conversation with you, so let it go."

"Since you wanna be so touchy about your *little friend*, I'll leave it alone for now."

"For *now*? More like *forever* because I'm not going to discuss that with you. I didn't even want you to know about it. Period."

"So, we keeping secrets from each other now?"

"No, I just don't want to discuss that. Anyway! Forget all of that. I'm trying to figure out why you were in my *bed* when your room is right down the damn hall. Why were you in my bed and not yours?"

"Well, basically, I was hiding from someone. I let a *friend of mine* come over one day while you were at work, and that nigga wouldn't leave after I gave him some of this good kitty, so I snuck out on his ass when he slipped up and fell asleep. He was getting on my last damn nerve, so I hid in your room until he finally left."

"You should've just told him to leave, dumbass."

"He's one of those sensitive ass niggas, so I didn't want to hurt his damn feelings by doing that. I might have to call his ass to come over again. Girl, the dick was too good."

"You are so pitiful!"

"I'm the one that's *pitiful*? So, which one of us is using an inanimate object to get off? It damn sure isn't me. Maybe if you get your shit together, tonight might just be your lucky night to get some real dick for a change."

"I don't have time for any of this shit right now, especially not the headache that comes along with trying to deal with these trifling ass men that are always out on a *Friday* night. Besides, I sure as hell don't want just a *lil' dick*. Been there and done that bullshit. Whoever said that shit about it's the motion of the ocean and not the size told a big hot ass lie."

"I heard that shit, sis! I feel the same way, and that's why you got to get out there and kiss a few frogs so the right one will find yo' ass. Shit, you might run up on a real *mandingo* tonight that can give what you got in that damn pillowcase some competition, so stop playin' and get the hell up. We both need to be gettin' dressed while you got me over here beggin' you to do some shit that you already know isn't negotiable."

"I'm not holdin' you up. You can leave whenever you want to. We both know that you don't need me to go out with you."

"Yes, I do! You know you don't want me to go out by my-self. I need my big sister by my side."

"No, you don't! So, don't even try that shit."

"Yes, I do, Britt! Besides, you know you need to get out of this damn apartment anyway, so you can find somebody to help you ease all that tension that's making you so damn mean. Think about it; *Mr. Right* just might be in the forecast for tonight. If you stay home, you'll miss your opportunity to meet him. You know you don't want to do that."

"Whateva! The way my life is set up right now, *Mr. Right* is just going to have to find me someplace else because I know it won't be up in a damn club."

"Shit, if you don't go out, where else is a man supposed to

find yo' ass. He definitely can't find yo' stuck up ass if you're sittin' up in this damn apartment all the time."

"Did you hear anything I just said to you? First of all, did I at any point even say anything to you about looking for a man at the moment anyway? Shit, you fuckin' enough niggas for the both of us, you *lil' hoe.*"

"Well, you ain't givin' up shit, so somebody gotta shake the walls up in this muthafucka. Now get yo' ass up and get dressed. You're wastin' my damn time actin' like a damn baby."

"I'm not actin' like a baby!"

"Yes, the hell you are, and you're supposed to be the oldest. You're definitely not being the mature one right now. Man, you're starting to get on all of my damn nerves with this whole show you're trying to put on. Stop being a *bitch* and go get dressed now!"

"Really, Karmyn? What part of going out *every* Friday night is being mature? Me staying home when I know that I shouldn't go out is what being mature is about."

"You might just be right, but I really wanna go out, Brittysh! Please! I promise this will be the last time I make you come out with me."

"That's a damn lie, and you know it."

"Yes, but did it work?"

"Hell no! Karmyn, I told you that I don't feel like going any-where tonight, and I definitely can't afford it. My student loans are suckin' up every extra dollar I get."

"Well, that was your choice to get in all that damn debt. You had other options just like I did."

"Girl, bye! I was not about to accept money like that from your stepfather. You and I both know that my momma would've killed my ass the minute she found out. Have you forgotten just how crazy Bianca Thomas would get any time I disobeyed her?"

"He was just trying to look out for you because you're my sister."

"She didn't give a damn! The shit our sperm donor pulled on her changed everything about my mother. I still remember the day she told me everything that happened. She told me that after he did her like that, she made a promise to herself to never let her guard down when it came to any man ever again."

"Bianca can't hold every man accountable for what one man did. Shit happens! It's crazy how she let that one situation dictate the rest of her life and yours too. Javier just wanted to help us both because he didn't have any kids of his own."

"I agree, but she'll never understand something like that. Your mother tried to explain to her a thousand times that Javier just wanted to help, but she wasn't trying to hear that shit. All she could see was that he was a man, so she couldn't trust him."

"I really don't understand why she felt like that. The man was willing to help you out because he knew neither one of us could count on our sperm donor. He wasn't expecting anything from her. You know money wasn't an issue for him."

"Yeah, but I think all she could think about was the fact that Javier was your mother's husband. Even though our mothers don't have any beef with one another, neither one of them will ever forget how they met."

"That's beside the point. Him wanting to help another man's children was what really mattered. He was more of a father to both of us than the man who donated his sperm to our mothers. Shit, I used to wish Javier was my real damn daddy."

"See, I can understand why he would help you. He married your mother, so it was the right thing to do. He didn't owe me shit, so I didn't have a reason to expect anything from him. I learned to deal with the cards I was dealt a long time ago."

"And that's why yo' stubborn ass is in so much damn debt right now."

"Whateva!"

"Just get dressed. The drinks are on me tonight if I don't find us a sponsor for the night to pay for them."

"Hmm...that's why that *twat* worn out now."

"At least it doesn't have cobwebs and dust all over it. That kitty between yo' damn legs about to die from suffocation because it's so damn dry. Oh, wait a minute. I guess it ain't dry, is it, huh. That kitty is probably just suffering from some type of nervous condition by now after feeling all that damn powerful ass vibration you be getting off from. You better be careful with that shit."

"Shut up and get out of my damn room now! I'll let you know when I'm ready, you red ass whore."

"That's *Ms. Red Ass Whore* to you. Don't take all damn night to get dressed, heifer. I'm givin' yo' ass an hour before I come back in here to drag you up out of here."

Karmyn walked out of my bedroom and slammed the door behind her. I wanted to open the door and yell a clever response to the shit she had just said, but I couldn't think of anything quick enough. Instead of dwelling on the situation, I headed towards my bathroom to jump in the shower. I still had to find something to wear, and I had no idea what that would be. Luckily, I'd just gotten my sew-in washed and curled Thursday afternoon, so I didn't have to worry about doing anything to my hair; getting dressed within an hour was going to be hard enough.

1 Hour Later......

Bang... Bang... Bang... Bang...

"You better be ready to go."

"Why are you beating on my door like a damn maniac? You

didn't even give me a chance to say come in before you walked your silly ass up in here. I could've been naked!"

"Whateva! I had to make sure you were getting dressed for real. You are your father's daughter, so you might be a good ass liar just like his ass. I didn't know if I could trust what you said. As far as I know, you could've been in here asleep. If I would've knocked and asked to come in, you probably would've just ignored me."

"Well, we both know what you inherited from him. I guess the *hoe* doesn't fall far from the tree. But anyway, it didn't even take all of that for you to find out if I was getting ready or not. As you can see, I'm already dressed. I hope you're satisfied now since you're so determined to make me leave this apartment tonight."

"I'm sure there will be a reason for you to thank me later. Trust me, I can feel it in my bones."

"Whateva!"

"*Whateva,* my ass! Look at you wit' ya' lil' stank dress on, I see you boo. That dress right there is screamin' to rise above them thighs tonight. You might just get you some *good-good* dick before the night is over."

"We both know that if I don't, *you* will."

"You damn right! I gotta have it, sis."

"Girl, you are a straight-up freak. You need to get some help for that issue."

"I get all the help I need. Trust me, baby."

With a huge smile on her face, she turned around and walked out of my room. I shook my head as I followed closely behind her. As I admired the way she effortlessly sauntered towards the front door of the apartment we shared, I silently desired to be as confident as my sister was. Unlike me, Karmyn has always been what I considered a social butterfly; she's consistently ready to have a good time no matter what the circumstances are. My baby sister definitely isn't afraid to live her life to the fullest. I'd always craved to be as uninhibited, but I just didn't know how to accomplish it.

"How do I look?"

"I just told you that you might get some dick wearin' that dress tonight! Trust me, that red is poppin' on you, sis. How does this dress look on me? I wasn't sure about it."

"You're gorgeous, of course! That green is definitely your color."

"Well, let's see if this green dress can bring me the *luck* of the Irish tonight, baby."

"You are one silly girl."

Before leaving our apartment, we both stopped in front of the huge mirror strategically placed right next to the front door to get one last glance at ourselves. There was no way that either one of us would dare walk out of that door without making sure everything was on point. I had to admit that we both looked good as hell tonight too. The lime green bodycon dress that she had on was almost identical to the red dress I was wearing; the only difference besides the color was that my dress had long-sleeves while her dress was strapless.

My baby sister and I were only 3 months apart, but the assumption that we were twins constantly happened when we were together ever since we were little girls. There were circumstances where we'd even been mistaken for one another. The resemblance between the two of us couldn't go unnoticed even if we tried to ignore it. Even though we only shared the same sperm donor, we were almost identical. Karmyn and I both had the same creamy golden skin that embodied a certain glow to it that many envied, while others constantly complimented us for having something so priceless. Our eyes were even the same hazel color. According to our mothers, we'd both inherited our exotic features from our sperm donor. Sadly, that only served as a reminder to them both of what they'd gone through with him. His two-timing ass was sleeping with both of our mothers at the same time without them even knowing. While Karmyn's mother was able to get over what happened, my mother never seemed to recover from his deception. Because of his antics, she never allowed herself to love another man; Miguel broke her heart, and I don't know if she'll ever get over what he did to her.

Miguel Sanchez is the man that Karmyn and I both referred to as only our sperm donor. He'd never been much of a father to either one of us. It never seemed to be an issue while we were growing up, though. Both of our mothers made sure we knew that his love wasn't required to validate who we were. When Karmyn and I were old enough to understand what happened, our mothers explained the entire situation to us. They wanted us both to be aware of the games men were capable of playing, so neither one of us would get caught up in anything like they'd gone through. It was obvious that it had taken a toll on them both, but I had to admit that my mother was the one who suffered the most. According to her, Miguel was her first love. They met when they were teenagers and quickly became high school sweethearts. On the night of their high school graduation, my mother gave Miguel her virginity to show him just how much she loved him. A couple of months later, she found out she was pregnant with me. He seemed to be just as excited about the news as she was, so they decided to move in together. My mother was so happy, but it didn't take long for that to change. While she was at home planning a future with him, Miguel was busy sneaking around with Karmyn's mother, Rita. My mother had no idea of what he was doing behind her back until he crossed Rita in the worse way.

Unaware that Miguel was already in a relationship and had a baby on the way, Rita was under the impression that he would be just as excited she was to hear the news about her pregnancy. She was sadly mistaken. Instead, Miguel got angry and insisted she have an abortion before he stormed out of her apartment. Confused by his unexpected reaction, Rita decided to follow him to wherever he was going that night once he abruptly left her apartment. She followed him from a safe distance to make sure he didn't see her. When she saw him approach a pregnant woman sitting outside of an apartment, she almost fainted when he kissed her lips. Hurt by this discovery, Rita walked home in somewhat of a daze as she tried to figure out a way out of the mess Miguel had created. The idea of aborting her baby was out of the question, so she decided she would expose him instead. She refused to let him get away with what he'd done to her; Rita wanted him to feel some of the pain she was experiencing because of his lies. In her eyes, he deserved to suffer as well.

Karmyn's mother told us that she waited until the next day to execute her plan. Instead of confronting my mother while he was home, she purposely waited until she knew he'd left for work. Rita then returned to the apartment she saw my mother sitting in front of and told her everything about the relationship between her and my father; she even told my mother that she was pregnant as well. It broke my mother's heart, but she respected Rita for telling her the truth. Angered by his deceit, she waited until he got home to confront him. As soon as he tried to convince her that Rita was just some crazy woman determined to ruin their relationship, she knew he was full of shit. My mother refused to allow herself to fall for his lies any longer, so she made him pack his things and leave their apartment that same night. After he left, neither one of them heard from him or saw his ass again; it was like he just disappeared. To make sure my sister and I had a relationship, they put their differences aside and raised us together. Because of those two women, we've always been each other's best friend. Karmyn was and still is the yin to my yang; nothing could come between us.

*****

"I be feeling like the man when I walk through... Ain't stunting what you saying when I walk through... I got all these hoes staring when I walk through... I done made a few bands when I walk through...

Watch me, watch me, hey, watch me walk through... Watch me, watch me, hey, watch me walk through... Watch me, watch me, hey, watch me walk through... I done made a few bands when I walk through..."

Rich Homie Quan's popular song *Walk Thru* blasted through the speakers as we entered the club. That song had every negro who thought he was somebody walking through the club as if he was entitled to wear a crown. From the moment I walked in, I regretted my decision to let my sister talk me into coming out tonight. I wasn't in the mood for any of this shit. All I wanted to do was crawl in my bed and snuggle up next to my body pillow while I slept the night away.

"It's so damn crowded in here. I can barely see where I'm going."

"Yesss honey.... It's definitely thick up in here tonight, and that's exactly how I like it. We're about to turn up in this bitch for real tonight!"

"Girl, it's too many people up in here to do any damn thing but leave. I can't even walk through the crowd without someone bumping up against me, and you know that shit aggravates the hell out of me."

"It's not that damn serious. Everything aggravates yo' ass."

"You damn right! I don't like to be touched."

"That's yo' damn problem. You wouldn't be so damn *touchy* if you let the right one touch that kitty."

"Whateva! What I need right now is a drink."

"I need one too."

"Look, both of the bars are already crowded. I don't even see any empty tables. If we don't find somewhere to sit down soon, you already know that I'm leaving. I refuse to stand up in these heels all night."

"Shut up! Don't start all that damn complaining now. Besides, I see an empty table over there. Come on before somebody else gets it. You shouldn't have worn those damn high ass shoes if you knew that you couldn't stand up in them long."

"If you're going to talk shit about me and my shoes, I can gladly go back home, honey."

"Come on, sis. We're here to have a good time, not argue."

"Yeah, whateva! You just don't want me to leave your ass here alone."

"As usual, you're right. Now let's just sit back, have a few drinks, and a good time, sis. We look good as fuck tonight, and these hatin' ass bitches already up in here rollin' their damn eyes at both of us because of that shit. You know you like that shit just as much as I do."

"Hell yeah! That shit has always been comical to me. I can laugh about shit like that all night."

Once we secured what seemed to be the last empty table in the entire club, we both sat down. As soon as my ass hit the stool, my bladder sent a signal to my brain. I had to use the restroom really bad, and there was no way that I could hold it any longer. I hated using public restrooms, but I couldn't get through the night like this even if I tried to.

"I gotta go the restroom. I'll be right back."

"It never fails. You always have to piss as soon as we get somewhere. You need to start wearing *Depends* or something."

"How about you kiss my ass. I bet you'll be wearing *Depends* long before I do if you keep allowing all these random ass niggas to run up in you. Somebody is going to knock ya damn bladder loose one day."

"At least I'll be able to wear my *Depends* with a damn smile on my face. It's all about satisfaction, sis."

"Does Momma Rita even know who you really are? I bet she

has no idea that the little girl she raised turned out to be some-body like you."

"Where do you think I get it from? She taught me every-thing I know."

"Don't say another word. I refuse to sit here and allow you to blame your whorish ways on your mother. I'll be right back, so don't move. If you lose this table, I'm going home."

"Whatever! Just go use the restroom before you create a real reason for us to leave. I wouldn't dare be caught up in here with you sitting by me smelling like a puddle of piss."

"Bitch, I'm too classy to do some shit like that. Besides, I wouldn't tell you anyway. I would just leave without telling you."

"If you continue to stand here running your mouth, we're both going to see just how classy you can be. Go to the restroom, Britt! You know there's probably already a line of bitches waiting to use it."

"Oh shit, you're probably right! I'm going... I'm going! Just don't lose this table."

"I told you, I won't. Hopefully, a waitress or *our sponsor* for the night will pop up soon. I'm ready to start drinking."

Without responding to what Karmyn said, I rushed away from the table. There was a private meeting in the ladies' room that I had to attend as soon as possible, and I didn't have any time to waste. I fought my way through the crowd as quickly as I could. When I finally approached the hall where the restrooms were located, I couldn't believe how long the line was outside of the ladies' restroom. There was obviously a meeting or some-thing going on in there that required the attendance of half the women in the club, so I had no other choice but to wait for my turn. I quickly took my place behind the last person in line. She was a short, big booty blonde waiting patiently at the end of the line for her opportunity to enter the restroom. According to the look on her face, it was obvious that she wasn't enthused by the circumstances either. At that point, neither one of us could complain even if we wanted to. I wasn't sure about her, but I had to use the restroom so damn bad. I had no other choice but to wait patiently like everybody else.

"This is ridiculous!"

"Yesss! It's been like this since I got here earlier. This is the second time that I've come over here. I figured that I might as well try to get in there now because it's probably going to be worse than this later when these hoes really get tipsy."

"Exactly! If I didn't have to use it so bad, I would probably just wait until I get back home. I don't like using public restrooms anyway."

"I feel ya, but I don't think my bladder is going to settle for that shit. I've already had a couple of drinks, so I know I wouldn't make it unless I leave the club right now."

"I didn't want to come out tonight anyway."

Communicating with the blonde chick that was in front of me helped the time fly by. Luckily, the line was moving really fast anyway, so I knew it wouldn't take long for me to get in there. When she finally got the opportunity to use the restroom, I was able to relax a little, knowing that I was next. As soon as it was my turn, I quickly walked inside the restroom. The smell that I was greeted with almost made me turn around and run. As bad as I wanted to just forget about the urgency to release my bladder, there was no way that I could. I was only seconds away from experiencing one of the most embarrassing moments of my life, and I refused to let that happen. I had no other choice but to hold my breath while I handled my business.

After finally relieving my bladder, I quickly washed my hands before making my exit. The smell alone was enough to ensure that I wouldn't linger in there any longer than I had to. It smelled like straight ass all up in there, and I didn't want to take the chance of that hideous smell following me around for the rest of the night. While I was so focused on trying to breathe in anything around me to replace that monstrous smell still invading my nostrils, I wasn't paying much attention to anyone in front of me as I quickly headed back in the direction of the table I'd left my sister sitting at. Suddenly, I ran right into what felt like a brick wall.

"Oops, excuse me!"

"Damn ma! All you had to do was walk up to a nigga and introduce yo' self. You didn't have to try to knock a nigga down on this dirty ass floor."

"What?"

"Oh, so now you tryna play like you didn't just bump into me on purpose. I saw you watchin' a nigga."

"*Whatchin' you?* Nigga, please! I wasn't even paying attention to where I was going."

"That's what they all say.

"Well, I don't know who they *all* are, but I can speak for myself, and I damn sure wasn't watchin' yo' ass. You sound really stupid for even trying to insinuate something so idiotic as that right now. This is the first time that I've ever even laid eyes on your ass."

"Yeah, right! Since yo' ass obviously tryna get at a nigga anyway, how about I buy you a drink. I ain't into allowin' females to buy me drinks. I don't get down like that."

Without being too obvious, I slowly examined the tall glass of chocolate milk standing before me from head to toe. His looks alone erased every moronic statement that had just come from his mouth. I could spend hours looking at him; this man was very easy on the eyes. Standing only inches away from me, his existence had unpredictable things already running through my mind. There was a heat captivating my thighs that made me want to slowly caress them, but I knew I couldn't do that in front of him. The last thing I wanted him to think was that I was really feeling him, especially after he accused me of purposely bumping into him. His ego would only grow bigger if he found out.

As I mentally debated how I wanted to respond to his indirect way of asking me to have a drink with him, I quickly remembered how dry my pockets were. That alone forced me to take his chocolate ass up on his offer. After looking at his sexy ass once more, I knew that I needed something to cool me down real fast anyway. Unknowingly, he'd just agreed to become tonight's *sponsor* for both my sister and me.

"The least I can do is accept your drink offer after having to listen to those tired ass lines you just polluted my thoughts with."

"That shit must not have been too damn *tired.* I see yo' ass still standin' here all up in a nigga space. It obviously caught yo' muthafuckin' attention."

"See, you're about to let your smart-ass mouth cause you to miss out on the once-in-a-lifetime opportunity to buy a drink for a woman such as myself and experiencing the pleasure of having me in your presence."

"Is that right?"

"You damn right!"

Completely shocked by what I'd just allowed to slip out of my mouth, I instantly felt embarrassed. Suddenly, I had a feeling that my unexpected arrogance was about to make him forget he even offered to buy me a drink. For some reason, I just wasn't ready for him to leave my presence. There was something about him that intrigued me. I wasn't used to situations like this happening to me, though. Usually, guys approached Karmyn when we were in clubs. I had been told on many occasions that I acted as if I didn't want to be bothered, so most guys didn't waste their time saying anything to me. Karmyn was usually the one who got caught up in circumstances like this. Unlike me, she knew how to handle it; men loved her forwardness. At this moment, I had to be channeling the *Karmyn* inside of me. Something about this man had me acting out of character. He had my complete attention despite the dry ass lines he'd tried to run on me.

"Keep runnin' yo' damn mouth, and I might just leave yo' ass standin' right here lookin' stupid. You better be glad you one of the baddest muthafuckas up in this bitch tonight."

From where I was standing, I could see the table where I'd left Karmyn sitting. I rolled my eyes as I searched around the room, looking for her. She'd already disappeared from the table, and I didn't see her anywhere. Knowing my baby sister, she was somewhere up in some oblivious victim's face trying to convince him to sponsor our night just like she said she would.

"You really have a way with words, don't you. I'm sure you've been cursed out more times than you can count."

"Nah, muthafuckas knows better."

"Anyway! Where are you sitting? Do you already have a table?"

"You damn right! My shit up in the VIP section. Why don't you come up there and chill wit' a nigga."

At this point, she could abort her mission because her big sister had obviously solved the issue. I had to find her first, though; there was no way that I was going to follow this stranger without her being somewhere close to me. It didn't matter how fine he was; my safety came first. Even though I was representing myself as being someone bold enough to handle the situation, I was far from that woman. Karmyn was the one who knew how to handle a scenario such as the one I'd gotten myself into.

"I can do that. Let me go find my sister first, and I'll meet you up there. Don't try to act like you didn't just invite me up there once I get up there."

"Nah, I ain't that type of nigga. Just let that big ass muthafucka standin' at the entrance know that you lookin' for me. I got you, ma."

Something about the way he said *I got you ma* caused shivers to engulf my entire body. He already had me under some type of spell, and it kind of scared me. I wasn't used to someone drawing my attention so quickly.

"Alright, I'll see you in a few minutes."

"Bet."

I felt like I was stuck as my eyes scanned his body once more from head to toe as I took in every inch of his chocolate physique while he walked away in the opposite direction. Even his bald ass head was sexy as hell to me. It had a glow to it that I'd never noticed on any other bald man. The manicured goatee covering the lower part of his face caused an eruption between my legs that I wasn't expecting. I'd never seen this man a day in my life before tonight, but I knew I wanted to see him again if it was possible. He had me feeling things that I'd never felt for anyone. Once he completely disappeared in the crowd, I woke up from the trance I was in. Suddenly, my sister popped up next to me out of nowhere.

"Did I just see you talkin' to that sexy ass nigga, Onyx? Sis, every bitch up in here tryna lay-up wit' that nigga, and you all up in his damn face like you know his ass."

"Girl, you know him?"

"Yes! Everybody knows him except yo' ass, obviously. He's that nigga to see, sis. Damn near every nigga up in this bitch wanna be his ass, and these hoes be tryna kill each other just to be in his damn presence. Don't you see all these bitches mean-muggin' yo' ass for real now?"

"Well, I had no idea who he was when I bumped into him. No wonder his arrogant ass was talkin' so much shit. He's walking around here thinking he's some type of God because a bunch of ignorant ass niggas and thirsty ass females are around here treating him like he's worth more than gold."

"Now, I didn't say all of that. Anyway, I found us a *sponsor*."

"Well, you can cancel that. *Mr. Onyx* himself just invited us to have a drink with him in his VIP section."

"Are you serious, sis?"

"Yes ma'am! Come on before he changes his mind."

Onyx

As bad as I wanted to turn around to get one last glimpse of who had to be the baddest muthafucka up in this entire club tonight, I knew that I had to play it cool. I didn't even know her damn name, but she already had my ass doing shit that I wouldn't normally do. She was so damn beautiful that she had me saying shit that we both thought was corny as fuck.

"Since you obviously tryna get at a nigga anyway, how about I buy you a drink."

That one bogus ass line played on repeat in my head like a damn broken record as soon as that shit came out of my mouth. That shit sounded dumb as fuck. Had me feeling stupid as hell, so I tried to play that shit off like I meant to say it. If I could have, I would've pressed rewind on that particular moment, but it was too damn late once it came out of my mouth. She'd heard that dumb shit loud and clear over all the commotion going on around us. The look that immediately appeared on her face when I said that bullshit was priceless. Shit, if I was a female, I would've quickly gave a bitch my ass to kiss the minute that shit came out of his mouth. Inviting her to my VIP section was my way of apologizing for the stunt that I had pulled to set up our little chance encounter. Without her realizing it, I was actually the one who purposely stood in her way to get her attention when she bumped into me.

She'd caught my eye the minute I noticed her ass walking towards that long ass line outside of the women's restroom. I was standing in the VIP section talking to my cousin Teddy when she caught my attention. I could barely understand what his drunk ass was saying anyway, so I welcomed the distraction. For some reason, she stood out like a sore thumb amongst the sea of people crowded around everywhere on the lower level. I knew without a doubt that I had to meet her ass, so I closely watched and waited for her to make her exit from the restroom. I had to be careful, though. The same blonde-headed chick that she was talking to in line was one of the many bitches I fucked with when I needed some pussy. Trina even looked out for my ass when I needed her to in the streets. She was cool as fuck, but she had a hard time accepting the role she played in my life. She just couldn't deal with the fact that we weren't in a relationship, no matter how many times I told her ass I was a single man. She didn't mind showing her ass to prove to me that she would do anything to win my heart, but what she didn't realize was that I wasn't feeling that shit. If she respected herself more, she would've already realized that she was just a *fuck* like all the rest of them bitches. There was nothing special about her, but she was constantly acting like she didn't understand that shit. I didn't want her ignorant acting ass to fuck up my chance meeting with this new prospect, so I purposely walked in the opposite direction of where I watched Trina's ass walk towards when she walked away from the women's restroom.

Getting my new prospect to agree to have a drink with me kind of surprised the shit out of me. She was far from the ordinary birds that I normally ran into floating around the club; even the way she spoke was different. For some reason, she had me intrigued. I knew I had to get to know her ass, and I was willing to break a few of my own rules to do just that. It was obvious by the way she responded to me that she wasn't used to fucking with someone like me, but I was on a mission to get her to consider it. When I headed back to the VIP section, the vibe she was giving had me feeling like I wouldn't have to put in as much work as I thought I would. Without even turning around, I could still feel her eyes on me as I made my way through the crowd. It was obvious that she was feeling me. I could see that shit in her eyes the entire time she was trying to front like she wasn't. She was sizing me up just like I was checking her out from head to toe, and I had to admit that she had all of my attention too.

I knew that every move that I made once I got her ass up in my VIP section had to be on point to convince her to give me her number. I had to see her again, and that was exactly why I had to get back upstairs to clear the section out before she came up there. My boy Rich had bitches of every flavor up in there trying to shoot their best shot to go home with either one of us, but I wasn't really feeling that shit tonight, especially after seeing her. She had all of my attention, and I wasn't about to let a few loose booty bitches prevent me from monopolizing all of her time tonight. This one right here was the type that you did whatever was necessary to hold on to her if she was willing to let you in her heart. I didn't know shit about her, but I could see that shit in her eyes.

"Bruh, we gotta get rid of these bitches. I just met a bad muthafucka downstairs, and I invited her ass up here."

"What the fuck that got to do wit' me? Shit, I'm tryna slide up in somethin' tonight, and this bitch Angela actin' like she really feelin' a nigga."

"Man, you don't wanna fuck that hoe. The tart ass smell of that bitch pussy got this whole area lit up. I don't know how you ain't smelled that shit. That muthafucka got to be leakin' or some shit."

"For real, bruh? I didn't know where that shit was comin' from. I thought that was some shit that was caught up in here from all the random pussies that's been up in here."

"Nah, that's her sour ass. Man, she been all up in yo' damn face and sittin' on yo' lap, so I don't know how you ain't figured that shit out. I bet yo' damn pants smell like her ass too. I hope you ain't been playin' in that sick shit."

"Hell nawh! But I was about to let her suck my damn dick right quick."

"Shit, her hands probably smell like that shit too."

"You stupid, bruh!"

"Man, I'm just tryna look out for yo' ass. I ain't got time to hear you cryin' and bitchin' to me next week when yo' damn dick about to fall off."

"Good lookin' out."

"Man, just get these hoes up out of here."

"I'm already on it. I hope ol' girl that you got comin' through got a friend or somethin' a nigga can fuck wit' while she up here. I ain't tryna sit back and watch yo' ass have all the fun."

Before I had a chance to respond to what Rich had said, he was already walking away. I shook my head as I poured myself a glass of *Hennessy* while I watched as he headed towards the entrance area of our VIP section where his brother was standing. They conversed for a moment before Deuce started walking around the area, telling all the females to leave while Rich stood back and watched. A couple of bitches tried to get loud with Deuce, but that was a bad move. I laughed as I watched him toss them both over his shoulders to carry them out of the area. They were cursing and screaming, but that didn't change the outcome of the situation. It only made the circumstances worse for them. All of that unnecessary bullshit resulted in them both being escorted out of the club by one of the club's bouncers. Deuce was always with us wherever there was going to be a crowd to handle shit just like that. He didn't give a fuck what he had to do to make his money. His primary purpose was to look out for me and Rich no matter what.

"You happy now? Ain't nothin' up in this muthafucka now, but dicks. This bitch better be bad as fuck, and she better have a friend wit' her ass, or I'm gon' kick her ass out too."

"Oh yeah? I'd like to see you try that shit."

"I'm just sayin', bruh. It's been a long-ass week, and a nigga need some pussy bad as fuck right now."

"You ain't got shit to worry about, bruh. I got you! Ol' girl got a sister, and she comin' up here too. If she looks half as good as the one I met, she still winnin', bruh."

"I hear ya. She better be. Shit, I need my dick sucked."

"I ain't got nothin' to do wit' that shit. That's on you to say the right shit to get ol' girl to give you some pussy."

"I hear you, man! I got this shit. A bitch can't resist a *playboy* such as myself. Let me do what I do."

"You do that. I'm tryna see what's up wit' ol' girl. I'm tryna tell ya boy, I got a feelin' about this one right here. She got potential."

"*Potential?* Nigga, what you mean by that shit?"

"You'll see in a minute. She walkin' in here now."

"*Damn!* Both of them muthafuckas bad. Which one mine?

I sat on the couch and watched her every move as she whispered something to Deuce. He shook his head up and down before he pointed in my direction. She was so beautiful that even Deuce's gaze lingered longer than it should have. As she casually walked towards me, I slowly stood up to greet her.

"I bet you thought I wasn't coming, didn't you?"

"Nah, I knew you couldn't resist being in a nigga's presence again."

"If you say so. Anyway… this is my sister Karmyn, and I'm Brittysh. I thought I should tell you my name too since you didn't ask me what it was earlier."

"Yeah, I thought about that shit after the fact, but I knew that I would get the opportunity to find out what it was when the time was right."

"Nigga, you ain't gon' introduce ya boy to these lovely ladies."

"No introduction is required. I already know who you both are, and that's all that matters. I know all about the both of you, trust me."

"Oh, so I see you got a smart ass mouth just like yo' sister. Trust me, you only know what a nigga want you to know. Now, I can't say the same for my boy, though. Rich can speak for himself, right bruh?"

"Hell yeah! The only way she gon' find out if what she heard is true is if she proves to a nigga she worth his time. Are you worth my time, *Ms. Karmyn*?"

"I guess you'll just have to find out, won't you. Anyway, are either of you going to offer me and my sister a drink? Isn't that what you invited her up here for, Onyx?

"Yeah, you right. I did promise her a drink. Ain't nothin' up in here but some *Hennessy*, though. Tell me what you want, so I can order a bottle for you ladies. You can have whateva you like."

"See, that's what I'm talkin' about. Order us a bottle of that top-shelf *Vodka* and some cranberry juice. Me and my sister don't drink that brown shit anyway."

"Oh, I see this one right here like to talk shit. A nigga gon' have to teach yo' ass how to act in a real man's presence."

"What the *fuck* ever! I'm grown. I say and do what the fuck I want to. Believe that."

"Why you so quiet, Brittysh? You ain't got nothin' to say now? Where is the woman that ran into me earlier? You almost knocked a nigga down and was still talkin' plenty of shit."

"Whateva! I'm pretty sure I can't knock you down, so you can save that line for someone else. I believe you purposely stood in my way, so I could run into you."

"What if I did? Do you regret runnin' into me?"

"I didn't say that. I believe everything happens for a reason."

"I think you might be right about that shit right there. Tonight, I was supposed to meet you for a reason. The only thing we can do is see where this chance encounter leads us."

"I guess we'll just have to wait and see."

6 Years Later

Brittysh

3:45 a.m.

Bzzzz... Bzzzz... Bzzzz...

The startling sound of my phone vibrating against the nightstand right next to my bed caused my eyes to suddenly pop open. Without disturbing the comfortable position that contributed to my restful sleep, I reached from beneath the covers where my entire body dwelled and quickly grabbed the noisemaker to put an end to the disruptive sound. There wasn't a need to look at the screen to see who was calling; I already knew that it could only be one person bold enough to interrupt my dreams. Without opening my eyes, I fumbled with the phone to answer it until I could hear the caller's music playing low in the background. Hearing Jodeci's *Freekin' You* was an indication of what this phone call was all about, but it wasn't going to happen tonight.

"Every time I close my eyes... I wake up feeling so horny... I can't get you outta my mind... Sexin' you be all I see... I would give anything... Just to make you understand me... I don't give a damn about nothing else... Freek'n you is all I need..."

"Hello."

"You sleep?"

"No, what's up?"

"Stop fuckin' lyin' girl. You know yo' ass was sleep. I can hear the crusty slob on the corners of your mouth cracklin' like rice crispy cereal while you talkin', momma."

"Shut up! I can't stand yo' ass. You say that shit every time you call me in the middle of the night. If you already know that I'm asleep, why do you ask me that same question every time? Why are you calling me this time of night anyway? You're disturbing my rest."

"Damn! If you don't wanna hear from a nigga, why the fuck yo' ass always answer the damn phone every time I call yo' ass this damn late?"

"I honestly don't even know at this point. I should've been blocked your damn number."

"Oh, it's like that?"

"It should be."

"You want me to tell you why it ain't like that?"

"Sure! Enlighten me as to why I'm so gullible when it comes to your ass."

"You ain't fuckin' *gullible*! You just in love wit' a nigga."

"Is that what you call it? Well, it doesn't really matter if I love you or not when the feelings aren't mutual."

"What the fuck that supposed to mean? You know I love yo' ass, so don't try me wit' no bullshit like that again. You hear me?"

"Listen, I'm sure that line works on all the other females you call late at night, but it doesn't move me. Love is an action word, so let me straighten yo' ass out right now. I don't love yo' ass; I just tolerate yo' silly ass because the dick good."

"If you wanna tell yo' self that shit, you go right ahead. I ain't gotta try to convince shit to yo' ass when it comes to how I feel about you. We both know that you love me, and I love yo' aggravatin' ass. You can save the bullshit you tryna pull on me for one them lame ass niggas you got all up in yo' damn face when I ain't around."

Silence filled the phone line connecting us to one another as I tried to figure out what to say next. I was left speechless, even though I'd pretty much heard him say the same thing on more than one occasion. At this point, I really didn't know how I wanted to respond to everything he had said, but I knew that I had to be careful with my words dealing with someone as arrogant as him. His silence was merely his way of testing me, but I wasn't in the mood for any of his games. Instead of entertaining his foolishness, I decided to change the subject.

"What do you want, Onyx? I'm trying to sleep, unlike your ass."

"Stop playin' around! You know I want yo' ass!"

"Whateva! We both know that you aren't ready for a woman like me, so what do you really want? It's been six years, and you still want to play games. It's obvious that you don't want me."

"Man, I don't wanna hear all of that right now. I just called because I needed to hear yo' sweet ass voice. Remember how I used to call yo' ass late at night, and you would just talk to a nigga."

"Yeah, I remember. How I could forget."

"I'm on the road, and I need somebody to keep me up. I'm tired as hell, bae. I been up for three fuckin' days. Shit, I can't wait to lay my ass down. Can I come get in yo' bed?"

"For what? You don't want to be here."

"Why? You got another nigga over there laid up in my spot."

"*Your spot?* Last time I checked, you didn't have a *spot* to claim anywhere up in here. The only person that lives here is me."

"Girl, I been marked my territory. Try me and bring another nigga up in there and see what happens."

"Do I attempt to control what you got going on at your house? I don't even question you about the bullshit you do. You're free to live your life however you choose, just as I am."

"Ain't shit goin' on up in that bitch. Shit, I'm barely ever even there, and you know that shit, ma."

"*Oh*, I know! What's that old saying? You don't shit where you lay your head, right? I know you're smart enough not to bring them home with you. That would be chaotic."

"What the fuck is up wit' yo' ass tonight? You straight doggin' a nigga like I ain't shit. Keep on talkin', and I might have to pop up on that ass when you least expect it."

"It wouldn't be anything new. We both know that's how you operate. Everything is always on your terms."

"I see you really ain't feelin' a nigga tonight, so how about I let yo' ass go back to sleep. I'm out here in these streets tryna handle my business, and you comin' at me like I'm some type of sucka or some shit. I ain't tryna hear none of this bullshit. I'll just hit you up tomorrow."

Without responding, I ended the call before he had a chance to anything else that could possibly upset me more than I already was. Onyx had somehow managed to call me on probably one of the worst nights he could've ever dialed my number. Just like he wasn't in the mood to hear anything I had to say, I wasn't in the mood to even hear his voice, period. Being confronted by one of his random strumpets while I was grocery shopping in Walmart less than a week ago was the reason for my anger towards him. I still hadn't gotten over it, and I wasn't sure if I would. Her squared-off manly-looking chin was etched in my memory. The way she carried herself was downright embarrassing. I couldn't believe that he'd stoop that low to entertain someone like her when he had better. After the way she acted, I could never show my face in that Walmart again.

Tired from a long day, I headed towards the registers to checkout. As usual, the only two lines Walmart had open with actual cashiers were far too long. I wasn't in the mood to wait any longer than I had to, so I opted to try one of the self-checkout registers. People were waiting to utilize those registers as well, but the line was nowhere near as long as the other two lines. I couldn't understand Walmart's scheduling to save my life. During the peak hours of the day, they rarely ever had anyone working. I'd considered just going to Publix to do my shopping, but I needed to pick up some cleaning supplies and necessities as well. Walmart's prices were much cheaper when it came to items like that, so that's how I ended up in this predicament.

As I patiently waited for my turn, I happened to notice some random bright-skinned female intently watching me as if she knew me. I glanced in her direction a couple of times to make sure I didn't know her. When I scanned her entire appearance, I knew there was no way that we were acquainted. The pale, almost see-through spandex jumpsuit she wore with a pair of furry slippers on her feet confirmed that. I was also pretty sure that I didn't have any acquaintances that would wear lime green hair on any day other than Halloween. Once she grew tired of just staring at me, I realized she was headed in my direction. The look in her eyes warned me that this conversation wasn't going to be a pleasant one, so I prepared myself for the foolishness that was about to invade my peace of mind.

"Excuse me! Ain't you Karmyn's sister?"

"Why? Do you know Karmyn?"

"Yeah, I know that bitch, but I ain't got no beef wit' her ass. It's her damn sister I got a damn problem wit', and I need to set that bitch straight."

"Well, I'm Karmyn's sister, but I have no idea of who you are, so I can't imagine what you could possibly need to set me straight about. I'm so sure that we probably don't even know any of the same people besides my sister, so I can't imagine what type of problem you would have with me."

"Oh, bitch! So you one of them uppity hoes who think she better than some damn body. I see you bitch, but just remember you ain't got shit on me."

"I imagine I don't, and I'm also not going to stand here and entertain whatever it is you think you need to straighten me about."

"Hoe, you know what's up! If I didn't have my damn grandma

up in this muthafucka tryna get her damn groceries, I would whoop yo' ass all up and down these isles about the way you been tryin' me. Stay the fuck away from my nigga, bitch!"

"Yo' nigga? Girl, who are you talking about? I don't even know you, and you have the nerve to confront me in a public place like this. All of this isn't called for."

"Keep talkin', bitch. You gon' make me slap the shit out of yo' ass up in this muthafucka. I'm tryin' real hard not to knock yo' ugly ass out. You know who the fuck I'm talkin' about."

"This is ridiculous. You're in this store making an entire scene about something or somebody that I probably don't even know or even would think about entertaining."

"Oh, you know who he is bitch! Does the name Onyx ring a fuckin' bell?"

"Onyx?"

"Yeah muthafucka, you heard me! Don't act like you don't know that nigga either. I know you been fuckin' him behind my back. My sister followed Rich's stupid ass one night after he left her damn house, and he went to see yo' hoe ass sister. It didn't take long for us to find out them niggas been fuckin' wit' y'all two wanna be saditty-ass hoes."

"Girl… Please tell me that you aren't in this store making a fool of yourself over someone I'm not even with. If you have a problem with who that man socializes with, you need to take that up with him."

"Trust me, I already warned his ass about fuckin' wit' you. I told his ass that I was gon' tag yo' ass on sight, so you better be glad that I got some other shit going on. I'll let yo' ass slide wit' a fuckin' warnin' this damn time, but if I find out you been callin' my nigga or tryna see him behind my damn back, that's yo' ass. That's my man, bitch! He lay up in my bed every damn night, and he know I ain't about to let his ass go."

"Is that right?"

"Yeah bitch, that's right! The nigga even asked me to marry his *ass, so soon he will be a married fuckin' man. Seriously, y'all hoes gon' make me kill one of y'all about my nigga."*

"Honey, if he's really your man, you shouldn't have any problems keeping him away from any other woman. Oh, and also, before you go around claiming a man, make sure he's claiming you too."

The look on her face was priceless when I said that. As hard as it was for me to keep it together while she embarrassed me in front of a store full of onlookers, I knew that I couldn't allow her to think she'd gotten the best of me. I was livid, but I would never stoop to her level to get my point across. No matter the circumstances, I would always remain the woman that my mother had raised me to be. When I looked back at the self-checkout area, I noticed one was finally free. As I approached it, I wondered what type of man I'd gotten myself involved with. He'd presented himself as someone entirely different from the type of man that would allow a woman like her to represent him. I just couldn't believe the Onyx that I'd fallen in love with would even associate himself with someone like her. I had to question myself at that moment. I wondered if I had allowed my feelings for him to blind me to who he really was.

Receiving that call from him caused all the animosity within me to resurface. Tonight was the first time I'd heard from him since the altercation occurred, and I was still trying to figure out how I wanted to deal with the situation. There was no need for me to interrogate him regarding who she was; I already knew that I wouldn't get the truth.

Onyx and I had been playing this back and forth game for six years now, and I was beyond fed up, especially after having to deal with something like I'd experienced. I was ready for a commitment from him, but he wasn't willing to give me what I needed. He always had an excuse. Claiming that we were from two different worlds and I was too good for someone like him was starting to get old. I probably should've moved on by now, but for some reason, I just couldn't. He was my heart. I wanted him more than I'd ever wanted anything in my life. Onyx didn't understand what I was going through, and I was tired of trying to make him see how much I loved him.

Brittysh

As soon as the radiating hostility that loomed all over my body had a chance to subside, I instantly fell back to sleep as if I hadn't been disturbed. Even though I was on vacation for the next couple of days, I still didn't want sleep deprivation to prevent me from partaking in any of my upcoming plans. Over a year ago, on Mother's Day, Karmyn and I had both surprised our mothers with an all-expenses-paid week-long vacation to the Bahamas, and they'd finally found the time to go on their trip. While they were on some beach basking in the sun, we were preparing to join them. They had no idea that we would be joining them in less than 24 hours, and I was beyond excited to see their faces once we arrived.

Our flight was scheduled to leave at 7 a.m., but I knew that we needed to be at the airport at least an hour earlier than that. I was used to getting up really early in the morning anyway, so I wasn't bothered by the time. Unlike myself, Karmyn had a major problem with it. My sister was not a morning person at all. To make sure we both arrived at the airport in a timely manner, I knew that I had to be up and ready to go by at least 5 a.m. just to make sure she was out of bed and ready to go on time. I even agreed to drive all the way across town to pick her up, so she didn't have to get up as early as I would have to. I loathed the idea of having to go out of my way, but I didn't have a choice if we were going to make it to the airport before our scheduled flight left us both behind.

It was situations like this that still made me somewhat regret my decision to move so far away from her a couple of years ago, but I knew in my heart that it was the best thing for me to do. Even though Karmyn was my sister and my best friend, we lived two entirely different lifestyles. While I was focused on establishing my career, my sister still craved the nightlife. Being out all night long and dating all sorts of different men was necessary to live life to its fullest potential, according to Karmyn, but I didn't see it that way. We were both almost thirty years old, and I no longer desired to be a part of any of that. I also knew that I needed my own space for my own selfish reasons, so I chose a location that was closer to my job. It was hard for both of us to be so far away from each other at first, but I quickly grew appreciative of the peace and quiet.

While I dreamt of having almost white sand between my toes as I walked on the beach and the ocean-front view from the hotel room I'd purposely booked, my sleep was suddenly interrupted again. This time, the disturbance wasn't caused by my phone ringing, though. My peace had been intruded upon by an unwelcomed guest. My eyes instantly popped open when I heard my bedroom door creak as it slowly opened. I knew exactly who had made such a bold attempt, so I remained silent. I refused to acknowledge his presence. With a disdain look on my face, I closely watched him as he removed the shoes from his feet before heading into the bathroom without uttering a word. I quietly listened as I heard the shower come on. This wasn't out of the ordinary for him; Onyx would always shower before getting into my bed, no matter what time of day or night it was. I waited patiently for him to emerge from the bathroom once I heard the shower water cease. When he finally walked out of the bathroom with only a towel wrapped around his waist, I fought hard to contain the aching between my legs. After the confrontation I'd experienced with the reigning *Queen of the Hood*, there was no way that I was going to allow him to touch me in any way.

Once he eased next to me in bed, I propped myself up on my arm in his direction. Tonight, he wouldn't get any sleep in this bed, nor would I until he was gone. I waited a moment for him to speak, but he didn't say a word as he laid next to me comfortably while his eyes remained closed. Just like my peace had been disturbed while I was shopping in Walmart, I was about to interrupt his.

"Onyx!"

Silence filled the room as I waited for him to acknowledge that I'd called his name. I knew he hadn't fallen asleep that fast, so pretending not to hear me only angered me more. With a piercing look in my eyes, I watched him as he blatantly ignored my attempt to get his attention.

"Onyx! I know you hear me."

"What's up, *baby*?"

"I need you to get up!"

"For what? A nigga tired as fuck. I told you that shit on the phone. Go back to sleep. I'll play in that pussy in the morning, ma."

"Get up now! I want to know why the hell are you here in my bed? Shouldn't you be at *your* woman's house?"

"*My woman?* What the fuck you talkin' about now? I'm too tired for this shit."

"I'm talking about your *little friend* with the *lime green hair*."

"*Lime green hair?* I ain't got no muthafuckin' *little friends* walkin' round here wit' some shit like that. You know me better than that."

"*Do I?*"

"Hell yeah!"

"Well, whoever the hell that bitch is, she made it her business to confront me in *Walmart* of all places to let me know that *you're her man*. She also told me that you sleep next to her *every night,* and the two of you are getting married soon. So, I'm trying to figure out why are you here?"

Unable to keep his eyes closed any longer, Onyx's eyes popped open immediately as soon as I asked him the one question I urgently needed an answer to. Instead of responding, he sat up and leaned his back against the headboard. It was obvious that he had gotten beyond frustrated by what he assumed to just be a mere accusation, but I didn't care how he suddenly felt. While he shook his head in disbelief, I patiently waited for his response. Before opening his mouth, I watched him closely as he rubbed his hand over his face.

"*Fuck!* I know exactly who yo' ass talkin' about. Man, that bitch ain't my fuckin' *woman*, and you know that shit. That's just a petty ass bitch I know through Rich."

"Oh, I know. She explained everything to me as she yelled at the top of her lungs in front of everybody in Walmart."

"I don't know why you even let some shit like that get to you. Man, *fuck* that hoe."

"According to her, you have *fucked* her on several occasions. Hell, it was even good enough to put a ring on it too."

"Whateva. You can believe that bullshit if you want to, man. I know where my dick been and where it ain't been."

"I'm sure you do, and I'm not trying to start an argument with you about what you do or don't do with it. We're not in a relationship anyway, so there's nothing to argue about. I just don't appreciate her *low-class ass* coming in my face talking to me like that in public. If that's who you want, I don't want to be the one that's coming between the two of you."

"Man, why you even comin' at me wit' some shit like that? You know damn well that I ain't fuckin' wit' no hoe like that. Shit, that bitch just tryna claim a nigga like me to piss yo' ass off, and the muthafucka succeeded. Look at yo' ass. You can pretend like that shit didn't bother yo' ass, but we both know better than that."

"Like I said before, we're not in a relationship, so I don't care where you stick your dick as long as you don't try to stick it in me anymore. I'm not trying to present myself as better than anyone else, but she's definitely not on my level. If that's the type of woman you like, I can tell you right now that I'm not what you're looking for."

"Man, shut that bullshit up. You so fuckin' green. You can't even recognize bullshit when it's right in front of yo' ass. That bitch knew exactly who the fuck yo' ass was, so she came for you. Shit, everybody know a nigga don't fuck around when it comes to yo' ass, and that shit right there gotta mean something to yo' ass. I don't give a fuck what she told yo' silly muthafuckin' ass; you should know better. Why the hell would I even fuck wit' a slimy ass hoe like that. That muthafucka just lookin' for a sucka to help her ass take care of all of them damn children she got cause she don't know who the fuck they damn daddies. I ain't even tryna get caught up in some shit like that."

"So, you're sitting here trying to convince me that just some *random female* is trying to claim you as *her man* because she needs a sponsor for her kids?"

"Hell yeah! That muthafucka got like seven of them lil' bastards runnin' around the projects stealin' and shit. Man, I wouldn't fuck that bitch wit' a sick dick."

"*Really!* Onyx, I'm not as naïve as you think I am. I have enough common sense to know that you're not going to tell me the truth about her."

"It's real fucked up that you really think that I would sink that low to fuck wit' a sack chaser like that muthafucka. You act like a nigga just out here fuckin' hoes cause I can."

"I wouldn't put it past you, and I know there has to be more to this situation. There's no way that someone would just assume that they're in a relationship with someone without having a reason to think they are. You had to have fucked her or something, Onyx. She might be tacky as hell, but she can't be that delusional."

"Man, I'm telling you that it ain't like that. Yeah, she tried to give a nigga some pussy one time, but I shut that bullshit down real quick. She ain't even on my level."

"I really don't know if I can believe you. Why would she do something like that if she already knows that you don't want her ass? She doesn't even know me."

"Exactly! That's why she felt like she could try you wit' that fuck ass shit. Man, you better stop believin' in random bitches. I don't fuck around like that, bae."

"*Oh really?* You think that I don't hear things about you? Remember, my sister, knows every damn body."

"Listenin' to that shit ain't doin' nothin' but fuckin' up ya mind. You need to stop listenin' to every fuckin' thing somebody tells yo' ass. If you wanna know something about me, just ask me. I ain't got shit to hide."

"I bet you don't. Do you really think that I don't hear things about you being with other females?"

"I'm sure you do. Shit, a jealous bitch will tell yo' ass anything to fuck up what you got."

"Oh, that's what it is? I'm sure my sister has nothing to gain by telling me things she's heard about you. She just wants to make sure I know what's going on."

"See, instead of them miserable ass hoes comin' straight to you, they send yo' damn sister to do their dirty work. Half of them bitches probably been tryna give a nigga some pussy, but they know I ain't feelin' that shit. Everybody knows a nigga got feelings for yo' ass. I'm fucked up about you, girl."

"Oh, come on now! Do you really think that I'm that *gullible*? Seriously Onyx, I know you deal with other females. I've always heard things about you being with so many other females, but I just don't say anything. I'm just trying to figure out why I allow you to keep playing with my heart the way you do."

"First of all, I ain't playin' wit' yo' damn heart, so don't say that shit."

"I can say what I want to say. I know how I feel about *what-*

ever this situation is between us, so don't tell me not to be honest when it comes to my feelings."

"You can say what you wanna say, but you dead ass wrong about that shit. I know exactly why you still fuck wit' a nigga. You know why too."

"Actually, I don't know why. I really don't understand why you always find your way back to my bed."

"I always try my best to be real wit' you, so I ain't gon' lie to yo' ass. Yeah, I might fuck off every now and then, but them hoes don't compare to you. Ma, you're my best friend, and I trust you more than any damn body. Don't nobody mean shit to a nigga like you do, so I ain't tryna let you go."

"Whateva! I bet they don't."

"For real, bae, they really don't. I'm tryna be real as I can be wit' yo' ass right now. I know you really don't wanna hear this shit, but it's true. Shit different between us. We from two different worlds, so you don't see shit like I see it."

"So, what are we doing? If you don't want to be with me, just be honest with me, because I really don't understand why we aren't in a relationship if I mean so much to you. This entire situation is so complicated. I don't even know how to explain what we have to anyone else, not even my own damn sister."

"You ain't gotta explain shit to no damn body. You know how much you mean to me, and that's all that matters."

"You say all of that, but you still can't tell me why we aren't in a relationship. Why am I not good enough to be the woman you want to be with?"

"Man, maybe it's because you too good for a nigga and I ain't tryna ruin what we got goin' on now. Puttin' titles on shit don't do nothin' but fuck up shit."

"You got an answer for every damn thing, don't you?"

"No, I don't. If I did, I wouldn't be sittin' up in this damn bed wonderin' why we havin' this lame ass conversation. I should've been up in that pussy by now since I can't get no damn rest."

"Maybe it's time for me to shut this whole situation down since you think I deserve so much better. Maybe it's time for me to find someone who does deserve someone like me, so I guess you don't deserve to play in this kitty anymore."

"Man, don't even try that shit."

Before I had a chance to protest any longer, Onyx snatched the sheet that I was using to cover up my body away from me, revealing the thin see-through nighty I had on to cover my bareness. He obviously wasn't in the mood to listen to anything else I had to say. I knew what he came over for, and he was determined to get it now. It was obviously a non-negotiable situation, but I had something else in mind. Sliding between my legs wouldn't be so easy this time around. I quickly snatched the sheet from his hand and covered my almost naked body before he could go any further with his mission.

"Oh no, there will be none of that tonight! How about you go get some coochie from one of them random thots you spend yo' damn time with when you feel like I'm not good enough."

"There you go wit' that bullshit. A nigga try to be honest wit' yo' ass, and you throw it right back at me. Bae, I don't wanna go through this shit tonight. Just shut the fuck up and let a nigga put yo' ass back to sleep, so I can get some rest too."

I quickly jumped up from the bed before he had a chance to pin me down. Tonight, I was determined not to let him enter my body. Despite how bad I wanted him to slide up in me, I just couldn't let him. According to the streets, that cookie monster had been in way too many jars here lately. If anything was going to change between us, I had to push for it.

"So, that's how it is? You wanna play games tonight? I see how you wanna be. I'm out!"

I watched him closely as he got up from my bed and started to get dressed. Silence filled the space between us. I was conflicted. I didn't know if I really wanted him to stay or go. It felt like my words were caught in my throat, but I actually didn't really know what to say. Without even looking back in my direction, he slowly walked towards my bedroom door after he was completely dressed again. I refused to allow myself to try to stop him as he walked out of the door. Once he was gone, I felt warm tears on my flushed cheeks. It was crazy how I was the one pushing him away, but his decision to leave made me feel like he didn't care enough to stay. I rolled over and willed myself to fall back to sleep; I couldn't allow this feeling of being rejected to hold me hostage, any longer.

Onyx

After I left Brittysh's house, I pulled up on my boy Rich. As usual, his ass was posted up in the hood, trolling for a few young bitches willing to give up some ass for a few dollars. My dawg wasn't the settling down type; I had to admit that he was worse than me. I knew he probably had something to smoke, and I needed a quick distraction to cloud my mind. The bullshit that happened between me and Brittysh had me in a fucked-up mood. I was getting to the point where I wasn't sure if I could do anything to satisfy her ass. She was everything a man needed, but I wasn't the average man. There were consequences to the life I lived, and I didn't want her to have to suffer in any way for my bullshit. Brittysh didn't understand that; all she wanted was my love, and that was something I wasn't used to. The entire situation consumed my thoughts as I inhaled the smoke looming in Rich's truck. His ass was already high as hell by the time I pulled up on his ass, so I needed to catch up before I found something to get into before I went home.

"What's on yo' mind, bruh? You look like you worried about some shit."

"It's Brittysh ass! I slid through to slide up in them guts, and she was on some other shit."

"Like what?"

"First, it was about some bitch confrontin' her ass in Walmart. You know that bitch Shanna you fuck wit' right?"

"Yeah, what about her ass? I know she ain't come at sis in no type of way. You know I'll fuck that bitch up in a heartbeat."

"Nah, it wasn't her. It was her damn sister. The one wit' all them fuckin' kids who been tryna get a nigga to fuck wit' her ass for a minute now."

"No! I know that hoe ain't do no shit like that."

"Yes, the fuck she did. Man, in Walmart in front of a bunch

of damn people. You know Brittysh ain't wit' no shit like that."

"I know! You need me to holla at sis to straighten this shit out. You know I got you."

"Nah, I ain't worried about that hoe. Brittysh knows me better than that; she just in her feelings about us being together. I'm tired of that bullshit. Shit good between us the way it is."

"Not to a female like Brittysh. These hoes out here would be good wit' some shit like that, but Brittysh the type of female who requires the real deal."

"Man, I can't give her that shit! You know that, bruh!"

"To be honest wit' yo' ass, if you really wanted to, you could. Just admit you ain't ready to slow down."

"It ain't that. I just don't want any of my bullshit in these streets to cause a problem for her. She ain't cut out to deal wit' this type of shit. These muthafuckas are heartless."

"I feel ya dawg, but you knew who she was when you got involved wit' her ass. You were determined to lock her ass down, and now you tryna pull back on her."

"Bruh, I really don't know what the fuck I'm doin' when it comes to Brittysh. I love her ass. Shit, I can't even think about another nigga tryna get at her. She just need to calm down wit' that shit and give me some time."

"Man, you better stop playin' wit' Brittysh damn feelings. That woman gon' probably end up killin' yo' ass one day."

"I ain't playin' wit' her feelings, bruh. She know how much she means to me. Can't nobody fuck wit' what we got."

"Alright, if you keep this shit up, she gon' stop fuckin' wit' yo' dumb ass."

"You damn sho' got a lot to say about me and Brittysh. What about you and Karmyn's crazy ass? Now that muthafucka right there might definitely kill yo' ass. That girl ain't right in the head. Her nutty ass might flip out on you at any minute. Shit, let me check my surroundings right fuckin' now. She might be behind a damn tree or some shit."

"Man, shit ain't even like that between us. She do what she wanna do. I just slide through every now and then to give her what she need. Ain't no love lost between us. Besides, Karmyn different from Brittysh. She ain't tryna settle down wit' nobody. That muthafucka fuckin' out of both pant legs."

"Bruh, I know sis ain't out there like that."

"Shit, everybody know about her ass except you and her damn sister. That bitch livin' a double life. We have threesomes and all kinda shit. That muthafucka is a fuckin' freak, and I'm enjoyin' every minute of that shit too, bruh. She made it clear from the jump that she ain't tryna settle down wit' a nigga. On the real, I believe the bitch like pussy more than dick anyway."

"Hell nawh, bruh! Maybe she just ain't feelin' yo' dick game. You probably need to step yo' shit up."

"Nah, it ain't me! These hoes out here fuckin' up other bitches about this meat right here. I know my dick game on point. Karmyn just on some other shit."

"Yeah, whateva, bruh. Well, I'm about to get up out of here. Adalis just hit me up. I ain't knocked her off in a minute, and I need my dick sucked."

"See, you still out here fuckin' up."

"Get you some business and stay out of mine. My dick game on point."

"Until that muthafucka fall off! Don't come cryin' to me."

"You don't have to worry about that! Trust me! You just be ready to make that run tomorrow night. I need you to come through for me on this one, bruh."

"I got you! About time you let a nigga do some real work.

I'll hit you up for the details in the a.m."

"This shit real. I already let my people know you comin' instead of me, so don't go down there bullshit wit' no hoes. Get in and out as quick as you can. Some of them muthafuckas don't know shit about you, so they might try you. I know you ain't wit' that shit, so let them know what's up from the jump."

"I'm ready, bruh! You just answer yo' fuckin' phone when I call yo' ass while I'm out there."

"That might be a lil' difficult. I told yo' ass I'm makin' a run too. I ain't never fucked wit' these niggas, so I gotta see how they work before I do business wit' them. I'll probably be off the grid for a minute, but I trust that yo' ass will hold shit down until I get back."

"Oh, no doubt. I'll chop it up wit' yo' ass about that shit tomorrow."

"Alright. Let me get out of here before this muthafucka text me again. She fuckin' up the mood before I even pull up on her ass."

"That's why you need to leave them hoes alone and handle yo' shit wit' Brittysh."

"I got this, bruh! Like I said earlier, let me worry about that shit."

I jumped out of his truck and headed over to mine. The conversation I had with Rich had me thinking about the move I was about to make, but my dick had a mind of its own. I had some pressure on my back, and Adalis was the perfect one to help me get it off before I had to get back on my grind.

******

As soon as I got off the interstate, I started yawning non-stop. Still deprived of a good night's sleep, I gulped down an entire cup of coffee as I prepared myself for the long drive I had ahead of me. Thoughts of everything that went down before I headed out of town flooded my mind. All of that shit had the potential to knock me off my square, but I had to remember that I was a man about my business before anything else. I could've kicked my own ass for choosing to go fuck with Adalis instead of taking my ass home to get some sleep that night. It was all Brittysh's fault, though. She should've just given me some pussy, and I would've gotten all the rest I needed right there next to her. Thinking about the things she had said to me before I left still weighed heavy on my mind. I couldn't even enjoy watching Adalis suck my dick after that shit. I just wasn't feeling it, so I left. All I could see was the sad look in Brittysh's eyes the entire time I was away. That shit could've fucked up what I had going on, but I didn't let it. I knew it was something I had to eventually deal with, though.

Suddenly realizing that I still hadn't turned my personal phone back on, I picked it up from the passenger seat of my truck and powered it back on. Messages flooded my screen one by one as I headed to my destination. There was only one person on my mind, but I didn't see any messages from her. Somewhat in my feelings, I dialed Rich's number to see what his ass was up to. It had been a couple of weeks since I spoke with his ass, so I needed to let him know I was back. He didn't let his phone ring twice before he answered.

"Yo!"

"What up, bruh?"

"Shit! You on point?"

"Yeah! Everything cool?"

"Cool as a fan. I told you I could handle this shit. I'm at the spot right now. You comin' through."

"Nah, bruh, I'm tired as fuck."

"I feel ya! I'll get at you sometime tomorrow to chop it up. You headed to the crib?"

"I think I might slide through and see what Brittysh up to. I ain't seen my baby in a minute, so it's time for me to pop up on that ass."

"I hope she got another nigga up in there. Better yet, I hope it's one of them *Latin* lovers. You know she like that kinda shit. Her damn daddy one of them Hispanic muthafuckas."

"Shit, I ain't worried about that. Brittysh can't get enough of this chocolate meat."

"You keep fuckin' up, she will. That's a good woman, man. If you don't want her, step back so a real one can get her."

"Who? You?"

"Hell nawh! I wouldn't do no shit like that. We brothers and I know how you feel about her even though you ain't ready to admit that shit."

"As long as you know. Alright, bruh, I'll get at you tomorrow."

"Bet!"

Brittysh

I watched Onyx intently as he quietly stood in the doorway of the bathroom with only a towel wrapped around his waist while droplets of water still cascaded down his bare chest. As he gazed into my eyes, a faint smile appeared on his face. The weary look in his eyes was a strong indication of his exhaustion. Instead of badgering him about his whereabouts for the last couple of weeks like I'd originally planned to do the moment I heard from him, I decided to just let him be until the time was right. He obviously needed some sleep, so I refused to deprive him of his rest this time around.

No words were spoken as he slowly walked towards the bed without breaking the lingering stare between the two of us. When he finally climbed in bed next to me, I exhaled. Without realizing it, I had inhaled my breath at some point and failed to release it until I could feel his presence close enough to me. Just as I was about to make sure he didn't need anything before he drifted off to sleep, he laid his head against my chest. The way he was acting had me a little perturbed. My heart all of a sudden began to anxiously beat as a slight tremble replaced the calmness I'd felt only moments ago. When he leaned his forehead against mine, our eyes met for a brief moment before he gently kissed my lips. Capturing this very moment in my memory, I closed my eyes just for a second as he rested his head against the pillow next to mine. The pulsating thumping of my heart slowly returned to normal as I fought to hold back the tears of joy that threatened to escape my eyes. As long as he was right here next to me, no explanation for his erratic behavior was required. Even though the situation that happened between us the last time he was here still hadn't been resolved, it was in the past now. I couldn't allow myself to dwell on it at this point. Knowing that he'd chosen to be right here next to me soothed any tension that may have still lingered. My refusal to allow this tender moment to suddenly disappear prompted me to position my body to lay on my side just to watch him while he slept. There was no verbal conversation required between the two of us as he attempted to get as comfortable as he possibly could before falling off to sleep.

As soon as he got comfortable enough and started to drift off to sleep, the startling sound of something vibrating caused his head to abruptly pop up from the spot he was laying in. I immediately became nervous as I struggled to quickly locate the culprit of the disturbing noise without him noticing what I was trying to do. I knew it was coming from within the pillowcase where I'd placed it only moments before I finally drifted off to sleep a few hours ago. The temporary satisfaction forced me to lazily slip it in the pillowcase instead of returning it to the undisclosed location I usually kept it in. I wasn't expecting Onyx since we hadn't spoken in weeks, so I didn't think it would matter. This was a secret I'd successfully kept from him for so long, but my desire to have my needs met in his absence had somehow come back to betray me all of a sudden. Completely embarrassed by this occurrence, I quickly reached my hand inside the pillowcase to end the vibration without revealing to him exactly what my secret was.

"What the fuck was that?"

"Calm down, it's nothing."

"The *fuck*! Whatever it is, that shit scared the hell out of me. I didn't know what was going on up under my head."

"Don't worry about it, baby. Just got back to sleep."

"Nah, I need to see that shit before I close my damn eyes again. I don't know what you got goin' on up in this muthafucka."

"*Really!* Are you trying to say that I would do something to hurt you?"

"Nah, you the last muthafucka I'd expect when it comes to something like that. I just need to know what the *fuck* you got up in this bed. It better not be one of them damn plastic dicks, I know that."

"What if it is? It's not like you're around every time I need to ease some tension."

"*Damn!* My dawg got herself some plastic meat up under the damn pillow. Hell nawh. Britt, I knew yo' ass was a fuckin' freak. You been holdin' out on a nigga. Let me see that shit."

"First of all, I'm not a *freak.* Sometimes I just have needs that require immediate attention. Besides, it's better than me sleeping around with a bunch of different men."

"You know better than to try me wit' some shit like that anyway. I just can't believe you never told me about that shit."

"I don't have to tell you *everything* about me. You don't tell me everything about what you do when I'm not around."

"Man, just show me that muthafucka, and it better not be bigger than my shit."

"No! I'm not going to show him to you. I can't believe we're even having this conversation. I'm so embarrassed by this entire situation."

"Oh shit! You around here referrin' to that plastic shit as *him?* Damn, that must be ya boyfriend or some shit. How long you had that muthafucka?"

"Stop asking me all of these questions, and just go to sleep Onyx. You need to rest, baby."

"*Rest* my ass! Shit, a nigga ain't tired no more. I'm fuckin' wide awake now, and I ain't doin' shit until I see that muthafucka tonight."

"Why can't you just respect my privacy?"

"You ain't got no damn privacy when it comes to me. Keepin' shit from me might get yo' ass yoked up in this bitch if you don't show me that shit now."

"No!"

"You do realize that I can snatch that damn pillow and pull

that shit out myself, right? I'm tryna give you a chance to show it to me on yo' own before I get mad."

"*Mad?* What do you have to get mad for?"

"Woman, I just found out you up in here fuckin' my pussy wit' a plastic damn dick, and you tryna tell me that I ain't got shit to get mad for."

"You're acting like it's a damn person or something. It's not even real, Onyx!"

"I know! That's why I ain't killed yo' ass for that shit yet."

"I'm not doing this with you! I'm going to sleep, and you better not wake me up. If you do, I'm going to put your ass out of my damn house tonight."

"I ain't even worried about that shit right there. You can act like you bold enough to try me wit' some shit like that, but we both know the fuckin' truth. If you didn't want a nigga to be up in this muthafucka, I wouldn't have a damn key."

"Speaking of my damn key! I think it's time for you to give it back to me anyway. You don't live here and probably never will."

"I don't give a *fuck* about none of that shit you talkin' about right now. You know I ain't going no fuckin' where, so you can save all that shit you talkin' up in this bitch right now."

"Oh, so you just don't give a *fuck* about anything I have to say, huh! I'm glad I know exactly how you really feel now."

"So, you wanna do all of this over a piece of plastic? You rather start a fuckin' argument about a fuckin' key that you ain't gettin' back to keep me from seein' a muthafuckin' fake ass dick. I got all the dick yo' ass need anyway, so I don't know why you doin' all of this."

"Just go to sleep, Onyx. I really don't want to do this right now."

"Nah, you and yo' fuckin' plastic meat woke me up and started this shit, so I ain't going back to sleep until I see this muthafucka, and I mean that shit."

Refusing to continue this never-ending debate with Onyx, I begrudgingly reached inside the pillowcase and snatched the vibrated out of it. His eyes stretched a little before a huge smile appeared on his face. It was obvious that he had plans to use this situation to his advantage. Some type of plan was already formulating in his head; I could almost see the ideas accumulating as he glanced back and forth between my eyes and the black vibrator I held, snuggling in my hand. Instead of questioning him about what he had in mind, I remained silent as I felt my juices dampening the panties I had on. My body began to twitch with excitement when he licked his lips. I knew what was coming next, and it was exactly what I needed. As soon as he opened his mouth to speak, my breathing became shallow in anticipation of what his request would be.

"So, that's what you been fuckin' that pussy wit' while I'm gone? That muthafucka ain't got shit on me, and I think I need to remind you of that shit."

I slightly bit down on my bottom lip as I watched him remove his body from the position he held next to me in bed. He quickly snatched off the towel that he still had wrapped around his waist while his eyes remained focused on me. The dripping wet mound aching between my legs throbbed even more as I gazed at the protruding tool standing at attention in my direction. When he suddenly grabbed my legs and snatched my body towards his, my entire body slightly shivered as my legs promptly draped right around his waist. Without hesitation, he suddenly ripped the soaking wet panties I still had on from my midsection. As he slowly massaged my middle core with the head of his dick, he used the juices that coated my plump lips to saturate it. This form of teasing was something I'd gotten used to him doing to prepare for his entrance. Enjoying every minute of it, I braced myself for his next move. As I patiently waited, he continued to taunt me without any remorse. When he opened his mouth to speak, I knew he had something different in mind.

"Don't just hold that shit in yo' hand like that. Show me how you use that muthafucka on that clit when I ain't here. I wanna see this shit."

Completely oblivious to the fact that I still had my vibrator in my hand, I stared at it for a moment. This was the first time someone would see the excitement this inanimate object was able to give me. I wasn't sure if it was something I was ready to share with him, but I knew I couldn't protest his request at this point. Instead of resisting, I clicked the power button on and placed the vibrating tool against my already throbbing clit. When he entered my pulsating opening, euphoria captivated my entire body with every stroke he forcefully delivered.

******

Perplexed by Onyx's decision to spend the entire weekend with me, I took full advantage of his sudden change in behavior. Unsure if this was just the results of his unexpected discovery of the secret I'd kept from him, I refused to do anything to interrupt our blissful time together. Being able to do the simple things like eating dinner and watching a movie together had always been what I expected in a relationship, but what we shared was something unexplainable. I knew he loved me, but he just hadn't mastered the ability to show it.

While he sat in the living room screaming at the television as he watched the *Pistons* beat the shit out of the *Lakers*, I was in my bedroom plotting. I knew the game had to be almost over, and it was obvious that he wasn't pleased with what the outcome was going to be. He was a huge fan of *Lebron James*, so I knew he was beyond pissed off that his team had obviously lost another game. The way he was yelling at the television, you would've assumed he owned the damn team. He was so pumped up, and I had the perfect plan in mind to help calm his ass down. I had a feeling that our little quiet weekend was about to come to an end; Onyx wasn't the type of man to sit around the house all day, so I knew he would leave soon. The weekend was over. I had to work the next day anyway, and his phone had been ringing like crazy all day. Even though I had gotten used to his typical behavior, something about tonight was different. I'd made up my mind that there was no way that I was going to let him walk up out of this house without feeling the power behind the adrenaline coursing through his body tonight. I needed to feel him between my legs once more; my panties were already soaking wet from just listening to the way he hollered at the *Lakers* as if he was courtside at the arena with them.

I turned on the television in my bedroom to see how much more time I had to wait patiently for the game to end. As soon as I flipped the channel to *TBS*, a loud buzzer went off, indicating the game was over. I quickly stripped down to my bare essence and grabbed what I needed from my pillowcase before heading towards the living room. Just as I was about to approach the area he was in, I heard him call out to me.

"Yo, Britt, I'm about to get up out of here, ma! I got some shit to handle."

"Not before you take care of a little something for me."

His eyes quickly looked away from the television and landed right on me. A huge grin appeared on his face as he took me in from head to toe as if he wasn't already familiar with my entire body. When he noticed what I had in my hand, he shook his head. My little secret had heightened our sexual session more than once since he discovered its power. He was beginning to enjoy what it did for me more than I did.

"Oh, so you tryna feel this dick before a nigga get up out of here, huh."

"Don't act like you're surprised."

"You know it ain't shit for me to bless yo' ass when you need it. Remember that shit too."

"Well, I need it right now."

He quickly jumped up from the couch and removed everything he had on except his socks and jewelry. The throbbing between my legs intensified once my eyes observed just what I needed to satisfy myself. The way he slowly stroked his erect tool made my nipples harden even more.

"Touch them toes, ma. Let a nigga see how wet that thang is already."

"Nah, playboy! I got something else in mind for tonight."

"I hope you ain't tryna do no shit that might get you fucked up wit' that lil' muthafucka you got in yo' damn hand."

"You know that I wouldn't try you like that. I just have something else in mind, so sit back down on the couch."

Hesitantly, he slowly sat back down with his eyes trained on me. When my eyes landed on the anaconda standing straight up from between his legs, I knew doubting my actions were the furthest thing from his mind right now. It was obvious that he wanted me just as much as I needed him. Instead of climbing right on his lap, I decided to stand on the couch first. I placed one foot on each side of him. My throbbing kitty was right in his face, and he didn't waste one-moment taking advantage of her with the tip of his tongue. As he toyed with my already erect bud, I felt myself instantly began to tremble. I wasn't ready to tap out just yet, so I quickly dropped down to my knees. Being face to face gave me a chance to regain control of the situation, but that didn't last long at all. Just as I was about to place my lips against his, he lifted my right leg up just enough to push his way inside of me.

Unable to contain the tingling feeling running through my body, I latched on to his bottom lip with my teeth. With his hands firmly on my hips, he slowly began to pound every ounce of his thick meat inside of me. In my opinion, this was heaven on earth, and if I had my way, it would never end. I was enjoying every moment of the pleasurable pain he was delivering to my body; no other man had ever been able to give me what this one right here was able to, and I had to admit that it was like a drug that I couldn't get enough of. I was addicted to him, and I knew that I shouldn't have allowed myself to get into this predicament.

As he ground his body against mine, I slowly continued to suck on his bottom lip. Suddenly, I remembered what I held tightly in my hand. Without hesitating, I powered it on before placing it against my soaking wet bud. Immediately, my eyes started to roll to the back of my head even more than they were before. I couldn't explain the feeling taking over my body even if I wanted to. Tonight, I was trying to reach unknown destinations that I didn't want to return from, and Onyx was the only man I needed to help me get there.

As I pressed the vibrating tool harder against my pulsating clitoris, Onyx's strokes started to speed up. He held on to my hips tightly as my body bounced up and down. Somehow, he managed to clamp his teeth around one of my nipples without slowing down his pace. He was sucking on my nipple like a starving newborn baby. I wanted to scream out in ecstasy, but I managed to refrain from doing so as my head fell back. The indescribable pleasure that captivated my entire body caused me to feel like I was moments away from losing consciousness. Unable to contain it any longer, I watched as my juices sprayed his lower stomach. As the moisture seeped from my swollen second set of lips, my head rested on his shoulder once he released the hold he had on my throbbing nipple.

Feeling my essence must've excited him even more. Onyx swiftly switched our positions. Once I was on my back, he spared no mercy as he pinned my legs over my head, pounded in and out of me. I was suddenly unable to catch my breath. It almost felt like an elephant was sitting on my chest. Everything about the moment was painful and also pleasurable at the same time. When

I heard him grunt, I knew he'd released his seeds inside of me. He rested his head against my chest for a moment as he waited for his heart rate to return to normal. I couldn't help but to notice that the rhythm of his beating heart matched mine. Experiencing something as trivial as that still had the power to make me smile, but I kept my feelings to myself.

When he finally caught his breath, Onyx got up. As soon as I fell all the way back on the couch comfortably, my body immediately slumped down to the side, and I laid my head on a pillow. I watched closely as he disappeared towards the bedroom. I knew he was going to get in the shower to cleanse his sweaty essence before getting dressed to leave. I contemplated following him, but I was too drained to do so. I felt myself drifting off to sleep, but I fought to stay awake. I didn't want him to slip out without me knowing.

When he finally reappeared again, he was dressed and obviously ready to go. With a smile on his face, he leaned down and pressed his lips against mine. I opened my mouth just enough for him to slip his tongue inside. Gently, I sucked on it until he pulled away. When he stood up, I noticed that he had my vibrator in his hand.

"You had enough fun wit' this lil' black muthafucka. I'm taking this shit wit' me. I'll bring it back when I wanna see you use it again."

I sat straight up immediately. I almost screamed when he threatened to take my toy with him. Devastated by his actions, I contemplated trying to snatch it from him, but I knew he wouldn't let me get close enough to him to get it. At this point, I knew I had to find a way to convince him not to leave here with something I depended on to ease my tension when I desperately needed it.

"No! Are you serious right now, Onyx?"

"Hell yeah? You don't need this shit."

"What am I supposed to do when I need something to ease my mind?"

"Like I said before, you don't need this shit. You should be good. A nigga fucked yo' ass all damn weekend. If that pussy still need some dick, I'll take care of that shit when I get back."

"I can't believe this. Your grown ass is jealous of an inanimate object. It's a toy for pleasure, Onyx. Wouldn't you rather I use that than find someone else to take care of my needs?"

"Don't try me wit' that bullshit. You know fuckin' better than to try me like that, and you better not buy another one."

"Just give it back to me, please. I don't even know when you'll be back."

"I'll be back before you need this muthafucka. I gotta go, ma. I'll hit you up later. Keep that pussy tight for a nigga."

"I really don't like you right now."

"You ain't gotta like me as long as you keep lovin' a nigga the way you do. Bye."

Brittysh

"Why are you sittin' over there wit' the stank face? This supposed to be happy hour, baby, so you need to get it together."

I slowly hunched my shoulders up as I tried to fix the expression on my face, even though I knew Karmyn wasn't about to let the reasoning behind my mood be an afterthought. I was trying to have a good time with my sister, but I had too many other things on my mind. I had promised her that I would go out with her tonight, and I knew that she wouldn't allow me to back out of our plans. We hadn't spent any time together in a while, so I couldn't disappoint her. It was obvious that I wasn't in the mood, though. All I wanted to do was climb in my bed and sleep the night away.

"Girl, I'm just tired as hell. I was running around like crazy all day at work."

"Lies! Now you know that I'm the last person who would believe that shit, right? You can save those lies for somebody else. Go ahead and get whatever it is off your chest, sis. I already know who this is about. There's only one negro who has the power to ruin your mood when he's not even around."

"Have you heard from Rich today?"

"Oh, I should've already known what that pitiful ass face was about the minute you sat your ass down across from me at this table. We both know that you don't give a shit if I've heard from Rich's ass, you just tryna find out if he said some shit about that black muthafucka Onyx."

"Just answer the damn question. I don't want to hear all that extra shit you have to say."

"Alright. I'll do just that. Girl, you know that I don't talk to that nigga in the daylight. We don't get down like that. It's too early for me to deal wit' his cocky ass anyway. That light, bright muthafucka ain't nothing but a quick fix to ease the throbbin' between my legs late at night when I can't find anyone else to take care of it."

"Stop playin'! You've been messin' around with Rich just as long as I've been dealing with Onyx. Now you're sitting here trying to convince me that you don't have any feelings for his ass."

"Exactly! I knew what Rich was about the day I met his ass, so I wasn't about to waste my time or get my heart broken. All I need is dick from that nigga. Nothing more."

"Damn, I wish I could say the same."

"Girl, we both know Rich is a fuckin' dog. Honestly, Onyx ain't like that, sis. You two really do have a good friendship. It's the relationship between the two of you, or should I say the lack there of a relationship between you two that's just so damn complicated."

"I know, and I'm so over this shit. I know he's not my man, but the shit he does just burns me up on the inside."

"What did he do this time?"

It's the same ol' careless shit! I haven't heard from his ass in almost two weeks again. He popped up a couple of weeks ago and spent the entire weekend with me, but then he disappeared again. He won't even answer his damn phone or respond to my text. He has no regard for my feelings at all. Everything is a damn joke to him."

"Sis, you already know how that nigga livin' and that's somethin' that's not going to change any time soon. It's either you deal wit' it or cut his ass off completely."

"I know, but I don't know what to do. This friendship or whatever the hell this is that's going on between us is about to drive me crazy."

"Girl, I really don't see how you put up with his shit. One minute shit is good between the two of you, and the next minute you can't even find his ass. You know that's my dawg, but you're my damn sister, and I'm tired of seeing you go through this shit."

"Honestly, Karmyn, I don't know how I put up with it either. Some days I feel like falling for him was the worst mistake I ever made."

"See, that's why I don't even try with these sorry-ass negros. I just rather get what I need and get ghost on their asses before anybody has the opportunity to treat me like that. Onyx doesn't deserve you! It's time for you to show his black ass that you don't have to sit around here waiting on his ass to come around. It's plenty of other muthafuckas that would love to have a woman as beautiful as you are. He better recognize!"

"It's easier said than done. I can't deny that I'm in love with Onyx, and settling for someone else isn't going to change that."

"I know, but you have to at least try. Maybe you just need to give someone else a chance. You never know. It might just make his ass straighten up and fight for you. Onyx is just so fuckin' selfish, and he knows that you aren't going anywhere. Sis, you need to show his ass that you don't have to settle for him. Look at you! Girl, half these niggas in this damn building are lookin' at yo' ass, and you're too damn blind to see that shit. I hate that you are allowing him to take you through this bullshit."

"Have you ever been embarrassed by your determination to have something? No matter what you may have said or done just wasn't enough for you to get it. All of the effort and time you put into it still wasn't enough; it still didn't work out. Well, Karmyn, that's how I feel right now. I gave him my heart, and it just wasn't enough, and I don't understand why."

"It was enough! He was just too much of an asshole to see that shit. Sadly, a man like Onyx has to lose something to appreciate its worth because he doesn't understand the value of something as precious as true love. I hate to say this, but I don't want you to end up like your mother. She allowed the shit that our no-good-ass father did to her to dictate the rest of her life, and now you're allowing Onyx to do the same shit to you. If he can't recognize your value now, you need to move on. There's someone out there that would appreciate a woman with a heart as genuine as yours. You just have to be open to give that man a chance."

"I don't think replacing Onyx with someone else right now is going to heal my heart. Starting a new relationship without figuring out how to deal with my current baggage only causes it to accumulate. Most women don't realize that's one of the main reasons why their relationships keep failing. You can't keep pushing your pain and misery aside without dealing with it. Suddenly moving on to someone new is only a temporary fix. That shit just continues to accumulate, and then you're around here wondering why you can't get yourself together. If you don't believe me, listen to the lyrics of Erykah Badu's song *Bag Lady*; that song sheds light on exactly what I'm trying to tell you. I just can't allow myself to be that type of woman. I don't need a new man to become the bandage for the scares another man left behind."

"Alright, *Brittysh Badu*! Girl, you just enlightened me on some shit I never thought about. Shit, no wonder you're one of the best therapists in the city. Now you just need to counsel your own ass up out of this crazy-ass situation you have going on with Onyx."

"I'll drink to that."

"That's what I'm talkin' about. Fuck black ass Onyx! Let's turn up tonight and cry about that shit in the morning, sis. We need to find a damn waitress to bring us a damn bottle."

Just as Karmyn was about to yell across the room for a waitress to request bottle service, a fine young man approached our table. His smile instantly caught my attention, causing me to stare a little longer than I would've liked to. Something about his eyes was mesmerizing; he could've easily been mistaken for Shemar Moore's twin brother. The only difference between the two of them was the fact that the one standing next to our table was obviously a shade darker.

"Excuse me, ladies. My apologies for interrupting your conversation, but I noticed neither one of you have a drink sitting in front of you. If you don't mind, I would like to change that. After all, we are in what some would refer to as a bar."

"It's nice to know we still have a few gentlemen left in this city. Since you're offering to buy drinks, how about you join us and have one yourself. You can have a seat right there next to my sister."

"A gentleman would never turn down such a generous offer from such a beautiful woman. It would be my pleasure to join you two. Honestly, I was hoping for an invite."

"It would be rude of us not to at least have one drink with you. After all, you were gracious enough to offer. By the way, I'm Karmyn, and this is my sister Brittysh. We can get more acquainted once we get a few drinks on this table."

"Don't worry about that, *Ms. Karmyn.* A waitress is on her way over here as we speak. The staff has a tendency to make sure you're always happy when you own the place, especially when you're entertaining such beautiful women. Oh, and by the way, my name is Amir."

"Well, *hello, Mr. Amir.* This is a very nice place you have. I don't think I've ever seen you here before, though, and I'm pretty sure that I would remember seeing someone like you. I come here all the time, but my sister hasn't been here as often as I have. Where has someone as gorgeous as you been hiding yourself? Home with your wife?"

"I see you're the *aggressive one* out of the two of you. First of all, let me get this out of the way. I'm currently not married, nor have I ever been. I travel a lot, so I'm rarely ever here. I've actually seen you two ladies here before. I definitely noticed you both on more than one occasion, but the timing wasn't right for me to approach you ladies, neither one of those times. Before you ask *Ms. Karmyn,* I'll just say that I was kind of in a situation that I had to figure out before moving on. Oh, and by the way, thanks for the compliment. I'm just curious if your sister thinks I'm gorgeous as well."

I caught myself choking a little when he made that statement. Before I could respond, a waitress suddenly approached our table. While he meticulously requested a certain bottle of champagne for our drinking pleasure, I tried my best to ignore Karmyn staring in my direction. I knew she was trying to get my attention, but I couldn't look at her after she'd just suggested that I find someone new to help me get over Onyx only a few minutes ago. As soon as the waitress disappeared, Amir focused his complete attention on me.

"So, are you anywhere as forward as your sister over there? She obviously doesn't have a problem with speaking her mind, and I can appreciate that. For some reason, though, her confidence only forces me to be more curious about you. To be honest, you're the real reason I approached you ladies. I couldn't allow you to leave here one more night without at least finding out your name and maybe even getting your number. I don't see a ring on your finger, so are you single?"

"Hell yeah! Her ass is definitely single, and if she doesn't give you her number, I damn sure will give it to you."

"Well, I guess it doesn't matter what I say at this point. *Obviously*, my momma has spoken."

"So, I guess it's my lucky day."

"I guess it is if you think so."

"I do. I've admired you from afar for a while now, waiting for this moment. There's just something about you that intrigues me. Your eyes have a sparkle in them."

"Wow. I really don't know how to respond to all of that. I guess I should start by saying thank you."

"That's not necessary. There's no need for a response. Just

know that I've had my eyes on you for a while now. I definitely like what I see."

"Damn. I don't know if I should feel offended or excited for my sister. After all, we do have the same eyes, and we're almost identical. As a matter of fact, most people assume that we actually are twins."

"Please don't be offended. You're obviously equally as beautiful as your sister, but there's something different about her. To be honest, I've actually heard a lot about you, *Ms. Karmyn*. Your reputation proceeds our introduction."

"I'm curious. What is that supposed to mean? What have you heard about my sister?"

"Yeah! What is that shit supposed to mean?"

"I definitely didn't mean anything disrespectful by it. I just happen to know quite a few men Karmyn has dated. A number of them are friends of mine."

"Oh, well, you can't believe everything people tell you. Trust me."

"I agree. If you don't mind, I would like to continue my conversation with your sister."

"By all means, please carry on. I have a phone call to make anyway. I'll be right back, Brittysh. I need to step outside."

"Okay. I'll be right here."

"Hopefully, I'll have something to drink sitting on the table by the time I get back."

Karmyn disappeared in the midst of the people mingling around. I couldn't believe that she'd left me in such an uncomfortable predicament, but I shouldn't have been surprised. I knew that I would just have to deal with the situation the best way I knew how until she returned. The *Shemar Moore* look-alike sitting next to me seemed to be a nice enough person, but I'd quickly discovered that he just wasn't my type as soon as he opened his mouth.

"Back to you, beautiful. I would love to really get to know someone as beautiful as you. If you're willing, I would love it if you would allow me to take you to lunch or maybe even dinner sometime. I'm actually a trained chef, so I could even cook dinner for you. It would have to be at your place, though. I'm in the process of getting my entire kitchen remodeled, so I can't cook for you there."

"You're already talking about cooking for me, and I don't even know your last name. Maybe we should try getting to know each other a little better before discussing anything on that level."

"Right! Slow down, bruh. You are moving way too fast for my sister."

I looked up and noticed that Karmyn had returned to the table to reclaim her seat while we were talking. Surprisingly, she wasn't gone long at all. The welcoming smile that she had on her face when he first approached the table had disappeared. Her normal snarky attitude had replaced it suddenly. It was obvious that his statement about her reputation proceeding their actual introduction had bothered her, and I understood why.

"I can understand where you're coming from. I just thought a woman like you would appreciate something more like that. From what I've observed, you seem to be a little more reserved than your sister."

"I'm not shy if that's what you're insinuating. My sister and I are more alike than you think we are. Please don't make assumptions before getting to know either one of us."

"It's nothing like that. I'm just saying if we spent a little time together alone maybe you would feel more comfortable. It could be the beginning of us really getting to know each other. You know what I mean."

"Actually, I don't know what you mean. What are you trying to say?"

"Wait a minute. Are you suggesting what I think? Are you already trying to get my sister to give you some pussy before we even get the drinks you promised us?"

"No...no, it's nothing like that. I just want her to feel comfortable around me."

"I don't even know you."

"Ironically, I was just talking to a friend of mine who used to work here. I mentioned yo' name, and she gave me the fuckin' exclusive about yo' ass."

"Oh yeah? Well, what did this friend of yours have to say about me?"

"The same way yo' damn friends told you about my reputation, she told me all about yours. First of all, you don't own this muthafucka. Yo' ass just work here part-time. She also let me know that yo' slick ass do shit like this all the damn time."

"What type of shit is it that I do all the time? Please enlighten me."

"Oh, I'm about to. My girl told me that you like to introduce yourself as the owner of this establishment to females that come up in here when you tryna get some pussy. Nigga, she also said that you don't even have a fuckin' car, and you live wit' yo' damn momma."

"I don't have time for this type of bullshit. I'm too much of a gentleman to deal with anything like this. There are plenty of women in here that would love to have a man like me."

"Well, take yo' ass to one of their tables. Your presence is no longer required. Bye bitch."

"See, I don't care for disrespectful bitches like you. Just loud and obnoxious. I guess shit would've been cool if I came for you, huh. You couldn't handle being dismissed by someone on my level, could you? That's exactly why you have such a fucked up reputation now. All men see when they look at you is an easy lay. There's no challenge when it comes to a bitch like you."

"Good! That's exactly what I want them to see anyway. Now get gone bitch boy."

"Fuck you, bitch!"

"Nah, fuck you! Hopefully, you'll find a slow enough bitch to let you hump on her leg tonight. You pencil dick muthafucka."

"Wow! I'm so embarrassed. Everybody is looking over here."

"You know I don't give a shit. These hoes need to know who his bitch ass really is."

"Let's just go now, Karmyn!"

"Wait! I still haven't gotten my drink yet."

"Are you serious right now? Girl, bye! I'm going home."

"Alright. I'll call you tomorrow, sis. Bella is on her way up here anyway."

I walked away without even responding to what she had said. All I wanted to do was get out of there. Embarrassed was an understatement for what I really felt. I have a very successful career, and I couldn't allow outbursts such as what had just transpired to ruin my reputation in any way. I'd worked too hard to accomplish everything I had so far. Karmyn never considered the fact that her actions could somehow tarnish what I'd worked hard for. It was situations such as this one that kept me from spending as much time as I wanted to with my sister now.

Onyx

I laid my head back against the driver's seat as I slowly drove around the dimly lit parking lot, searching for an empty spot. Tired from running the streets all damn day, I knew that what I really needed to do was go somewhere and lay my ass down before I allowed someone to catch me slipping. Instead of doing that shit, I chose to do the opposite. When I hit my boy Rich up earlier, I let his ass convince me to go to some damn club that I hadn't heard of with his ass. Some bitch he was fucking with invited his ass to a party she was hosting. He had been fucking with her on the low for a minute now, so he had to show his face if he expected to get some pussy tonight.

Now here I was in unfamiliar territory trying to fuck with some young bitch I'd only met a couple of hours ago. She was all over my ass from the moment I stepped in the club like I was a celebrity or some shit. The bitch was practically begging me to fuck her ass. She let me know that she was down for whatever too, so I figured it was the least that I could do to calm her ass down. Shit, I needed my dick sucked anyway. Normally, I didn't fuck around like this; I usually rolled solo, but I was willing to make an exception for my boy since the bitch he was trying to fuck was her roommate.

"Man, you know I love you like a fuckin' brother, right."

"Yeah!"

"That's why I need to be real wit' yo' ass, bruh."

"What the fuck yo' drunk ass talkin' about."

"Nigga, I'm tryna help yo' ass. I don't think yo' ass need to fuck wit' ol' girl. She might be trouble, and I ain't tryna get involved in that shit."

"You got me way over here, and now you tryna tell me this muthafucka might be trouble. What do you mean? Speak on that shit before I park my fuckin' truck."

"Bruh, I just don't want Brittysh to find this shit out. She might kill my ass if she finds out I had yo' ass over here fuckin' wit' another bitch behind her back."

"Hold up! Is yo' ass worried about Brittysh finding out, or is it Karmyn you tryna hide this shit from?"

"I keep tellin' you that shit ain't like that between me and Karmyn. That muthafucka ain't tryna fuck wit' a nigga like that. I don't hear from her ass until she wanna fuck."

"So, you just another nigga in rotation?"

"Hell yeah, and I'm good wit' that shit. But I know Brittysh ain't feelin' no shit like that. She loves yo' ass, and you know that shit."

"That ain't nothin' you need to worry about. Fuckin' this bitch don't change shit for me. Brittysh ain't going nowhere. She know these hoes don't mean shit to me."

"Keep on, bruh! I'm tryna tell you this shit gon' blow up in yo' fuckin' face one damn day."

As soon as he said that shit, I pulled in a park. Before I could respond to the bullshit, he said, the bitch that was desperately trying to get me to fuck her started tapping on my damn window. I immediately looked in her direction, so she could see the aggravation I felt all over my face. Her antics were already making me reconsider my decision to fuck with her. When she recognized my frustration, she immediately stopped tapping on my window. Curious to find out why she so desperately needed to speak to me at that moment, I opened my door to see what she had to say.

"Yo! What's up?"

"Y'all comin' upstairs, right?"

"Yeah! Give us a minute. Bruh, know where you at, right?"

"Yess! I just wanted to make sure you ain't leavin' before you come to see me."

Without responding, I closed my door in her face. This bitch was becoming a little too needy for me, and I wasn't feeling that shit. She was acting like she had some shit up her damn sleeve. I didn't know if this bitch was trying to set my ass up or some shit. When she finally walked away from my door, I looked at Rich and shook my head.

"Bruh, you know I ain't feelin' that shit. I ain't got time for no needy muthafucka."

"I feel ya, bruh! Yeah, she doin' a little too damn much. If you do run-up in that, you probably wanna strap up twice. She might be tryna trap a nigga for real."

"Shit, the way she actin' her ass better be glad if I let her ass suck my damn dick."

"I feel ya, bruh!"

"Let me go up here and see what the fuck she talkin' about. Shit, I might fall asleep on her ass. I'm tired as fuck."

I grabbed my keys before I stepped out of my truck. When Rich closed the passenger door after he got out, I hit the button on my key fob to lock my doors as I walked towards the apartment building. As soon as my right foot hit the first step, I felt my personal phone vibrating in my pocket. I immediately felt the weight of the world on my shoulders. My instincts had me feeling like I was about to hear some shit that I didn't want to hear. I pulled the phone out of my pocket to see who was calling before the caller hung up. When I saw the word *momma* flashing on the screen, I stopped dead in my tracks before answering her call. I automatically knew it had to be an emergency for her to call me this time of night. As soon as I slid the green icon across the screen, all I heard was her screaming and crying. Without saying a word, I turned around and headed back towards my truck.

"What's wrong, ma?"

"My baby...."

"What's going on? I need you to calm down and talk to me."

"He's gone! My baby gone."

"What? Tell me what's going on now! Where you at?"

"I'm at the hospital."

Brittysh

The sudden feeling of a presence sitting on the other side of my bed startled me. Fear immediately captivated my soul as I slightly opened my eyes to observe my surroundings. Silently praying this uncanny feeling was just the afterthought of a nightmare I was having, I prepared myself for the possibility of this disturbance being a part of my reality. My eyes suddenly landing on what seemed to be someone sitting on the edge of the bed with their head hanging low in what I presumed to be despair. No longer unsure of the presence looming in my bedroom, I moved closer to the figure. The sound of sniffling alerted me that something was definitely wrong.

"Onyx? Are you alright?"

The disturbing sound of his constant sniffling remained the only sound looming in the space we shared. His emotional state had him speechless. I waited patiently to give him a chance to speak, but still, he said nothing. I watched him from behind as he continued to shed tears. My heart ached as his misery consumed him right before my eyes. Unable to wait any longer, I attempted to get him to tell me what had him so overwhelmed again.

"Onyx baby, what's wrong? Talk to me, please."

I tried to wrap my arms around him, but he quickly pulled away. I wasn't used to him being so guarded when he was in my presence. Everything about his demeanor had me feeling uneasy all of a sudden. Seeing the man that I was in love with in this condition was unordinary; he was obviously in turmoil, and I had no idea of what to do. Onyx's unwillingness to be comforted at a time when he obviously needed it the most caused me to feel a little leery of what could've occurred to push him to this point.

I watched him closely as I sat in silence, waiting on him to divulge the details of the tragedy surrounding the pain he was experiencing right before my eyes. His entire body trembled as he continued to weep uncontrollably. At that moment, I felt completely helpless. I wanted to do more, but he wouldn't allow me to touch him at this point. Sadly, I was unaware of how I should react in these circumstances. No matter how hard I tried to figure it out on my own, I just wasn't sure of what could've happened to send him here in this state of mind. I wanted so badly to hold him close in my arms. Right now, I just needed Onyx to know that I was here for him no matter what was going on. Instead of attempting to try to hold him in my arms again, I climbed out of bed and sat next to him on the edge of the bed so that he could feel my presence. As soon as he felt me close to him, I noticed how his body relaxed somewhat. He looked as if the weight of the world was on his shoulders, and I didn't know how I could contribute to making any of the circumstances surrounding him any better.

I waited for what seemed like an eternity to give Onyx the opportunity to open up to me. I knew him well enough not to attempt to force him to do anything he didn't want to do; that would only push him farther away. As I sat there in silence, I noticed that his weeping had all of a sudden ceased. The moment his body slumped deeper in the spot he sat in, he finally wiped away the remaining tears falling from his eyes. I had a feeling he was ready to speak, so I braced myself as much as I could to prepare for whatever he had to say.

"He gone!"

"Who Onyx?"

"My lil' brother! He gone!"

"Oh my god! What happened?"

"He got hit by a fuckin' truck! Damn, I still can't believe this shit! That nigga dead, and it's my fuckin' fault."

"What do you mean it's *your fault*, baby?"

"That lil' nigga talked me into buyin' his ass a fuckin' motorcycle for his damn birthday last month. I knew I shouldn't have got him that shit. Damn, my momma told me not to buy his ass that fuckin' bike too. I should've listened to her ass! Man, I should've respected where my ol' girl was comin' from. I fucked up, baby! I fucked up!"

"I know your pain won't allow you to understand what I'm trying to say to you right now, but this is not your fault Onyx. You were just trying to be a good brother and make him happy."

"Yeah, you right! That's some shit I don't wanna hear right now and it damn sho' ain't gon' bring my fuckin' brother back."

"I'm not trying to upset you. Please, calm down. I'm just trying to be here for you, baby!"

"Well, you damn sho' ain't doin' a fuckin' good job of that shit! You talkin' out yo' ass right now tryna convince me this shit ain't my fuckin' fault. I bought that nigga that *fuckin'* bike, Brittysh!"

He jumped up from the bed. His chest was heaving up and down as a rush of adrenaline coursed through his veins. I'd never seen him so angry, but I knew Onyx well enough to know that I didn't have to be in fear.

"Onyx, I'm sure your mother doesn't blame you for the accident your brother was in."

"Man, you talkin' crazy right now! For real, ma! You think my momma wanna hear that bullshit you talkin' when she gotta bury her baby boy. That nigga was the only thing she had to be proud of cause she know I ain't shit! He was in college! My brother was gon' be a fuckin' doctor. He was all she could count on. I ain't nothing but a fuckin' drug dealer."

"Stop talking like that! I know your mother loves you just as much as she loves your brother. I'm sure the choices you made didn't change how she felt about you."

"I ain't say she didn't love me! She just know I ain't shit! The one son she got left gon' either end up dead in these streets or in prison. My fuckin' brother was her only hope. He was the main reason I was in these streets grindin' so damn hard. I pushed that nigga to be all he can be, so she would have at least one son who was worth something. I know you can't understand that shit! You didn't grow up like we grew up. Shit was sweet for you!"

"That's not fair, Onyx! I do understand what you're saying. My life wasn't as wonderful as you think it was. My mother struggled too. She pushed me to be better than her, just like you pushed your brother."

"Man, I gotta get out of here! I don't know why I even came here. I knew you wouldn't see this shit like me. You don't understand a nigga, and you never will. This shit right here is exactly why I can't be wit' yo' ass. No matter how hard I try, I can't get you to see that shit is real out here. Everybody can't live in a fuckin' perfect world like yo' ass. Shit is all fucked up now! I ain't got love for no muthafucka now. I'm ready to accept what's comin' for me. My life ain't worth shit without my damn brother. A nigga can't be nothin' but a cold muthafucka now."

Tears began to cascade down my warm cheeks as I listened to Onyx blatantly dismiss any feelings he'd ever had for me. I knew he was grieving the loss of his brother, but I couldn't help but to feel like he meant every word he'd said. To hear him admit his reasons for not being with me penetrated my soul instantly. I felt my heart slowly breaking as I realized I was in love with a man who would never love me the way I loved him. I had to accept there was nothing I could do to save Onyx anymore; he had to want it for himself.

For the first time, I had to admit that maybe he was right. Maybe Onyx knew what he was talking about when he said the lifestyles we each lived would always cause a certain void between us. While I was trying to love him through his pain and convince him that he could be a better man, all along, he was willing to just accept his circumstances and what he was destined for. It was obvious Onyx didn't want any more than what he already had; he had convinced himself that he wasn't worthy of anything more. My love didn't matter enough to him, and there was nothing I could do to change that. No matter what I tried to do to convince him that I would always be here for him through any circumstances, it would never be enough because he didn't understand that type of love.

As I sat on the side of my bed silently, I watched him intently as he continued to pace back and forth. His anger continued to manifest right before my eyes. It was clear that he didn't desire my love at this moment, so I no longer tried to force myself on him. When he finally grew tired of the limited space in which he had to tread back and forth, he finally walked out of my bedroom without so much as one word spoken to me. At that moment, something within me wondered if this was how it was supposed to be; maybe Onyx just wasn't meant to be a part of my life as I may have desired.

******

I hadn't heard from Onyx since he stormed out of my bedroom over a week ago. I wanted to reach out to him just to check on his well-being after the death of his brother, but for some reason, I just couldn't. Something had changed within my soul since the last time we saw each other. Deep inside, I wanted to believe he only spoke the words he said to me in anger, but I still couldn't forget them. My heart ached for him in the circumstances he was dealing with, but I also had to realize that it was the dose of reality I needed to face what we really shared. Determined to focus on what was best for me, I did everything I could think of to distract myself from thinking of him.

It was way past my bedtime, but I couldn't sleep. Instead, I laid across my bed, scanning through the collection of pictures on my phone, determined to find a certain screenshot I took of a bad ass yellow blazer I ran across online. I couldn't remember the particular boutique I was looking at when I saw it, so I was hoping the picture would provide me with enough information to figure it out. It had been a long week for me, mostly emotionally, because my heart was still aching. Trying to get over a broken heart was easier said than done. I knew it would take some time for me to heal; it was just something I would have to deal with. Hopefully, what I felt would fade over time, and I would find someone new to love me just as much as I loved Onyx.

Tonight, I wasn't in the mood to do much else but some retail therapy online to relax my mind. I was in desperate need of something to monopolize my thoughts; I definitely didn't want to dwell on the situation between Onyx and me. I had given him and the circumstances surrounding the relationship between us enough of my time already. The idea of giving my heart to someone who would mistreat me was agonizing, but there was nothing I could do to change the past. Now, I just needed to get over him and move on.

As aggravating as it was beginning to get to concentrate on searching through numerous pictures to find this one particular screenshot I was looking for, I still somehow managed to focus my mind on seeing myself wearing the yellow blazer instead of wondering about Onyx. I continued to scan through the pictures for what seemed like hours, determined to find that screenshot. I knew that blazer would pop against my creamy caramel skin, so I had to have it. Karmyn was definitely going to be jealous as hell the moment she laid eyes on me in such a bright color. As I continued to slowly scan through my phone, I was trying to figure out how the hell I had so much time to take so many damn pictures. I found so many random pictures of Karmyn on my phone, and I knew she was the culprit behind them, though. A lot of them were also selfies I'd taken in my car or at my desk. It was definitely obvious that I loved myself; I couldn't get enough of the woman I'd become.

After admiring myself in the red top I had on last Tuesday, I swiped my finger across the screen to look at the next picture. The moment my eyes landed on my best friend, the blood running through my veins started to get warm. Onyx Jackson was the sexiest dark chocolate man I'd ever met. As I stared at the picture I'd taken of him lying in my bed asleep months ago, I thought of the night that I first laid eyes on this man. A smile quickly appeared on my face as I thought about the moment I bumped into him in a club over six years ago. The minute he opened his mouth once we collided, I should've run in the opposite direction as fast as I could. If only I would've known better.

"Oops, excuse me!"

"Damn ma! All you had to do was walk up to a nigga and introduce yo' self. You didn't have to try to knock a nigga down on this dirty ass floor."

"What?"

"Oh, so now you tryna play like you didn't just bump into me on purpose. I saw you watchin' a nigga."

"Whatchin' you? Nigga, please! I wasn't even paying attention to where I was going."

"That's what they all say.

"Well, I don't know who they all are, but I can speak for myself, and I damn sure wasn't watchin' yo' ass. You sound real stupid for even trying to insinuate something so idiotic as that right now. This is the first time that I've ever even laid eyes on your ass."

"Yeah, right! Since yo' ass obviously tryna get at a nigga anyway, how about I buy you a drink. I ain't into allowin' females to buy me drinks. I don't get down like that."

Without being too obvious, I slowly examined the tall glass of chocolate milk standing before me from head to toe. His looks alone erased every moronic statement that had just come from his mouth. I could spend hours looking at him; this man was very easy on the eyes. Standing only inches away from me, his existence had unpredictable things already running through my mind. There was a heat captivating my thighs that made me want to slowly caress them, but I knew I couldn't do that in front of him. The last thing I wanted him to think was that I was really feeling him, especially after he accused me of purposely bumping into him. His ego would only grow bigger if he found out.

Even though his lines were beyond corny, in my opinion, something about that man intrigued me. When he invited me to his VIP section for a drink, I couldn't resist his invitation. That night, we ended up talking for hours; somehow, he was able to become a permanent fixture in my life after that. He wasn't my man, but I knew him well enough to know that if I met someone, he wouldn't stop until he ruined it. He was really possessive when it came to me for some reason, but a commitment between the two of us wasn't possible, according to him. Now I was trying to find my way out of the situation we'd created; he wasn't going to change, so I knew it was time for me to move on.

Determined to continue my search for the yellow blazer, I quickly swiped left to move on to the next picture. Dwelling on what we could have been was something I just wasn't willing to do anymore. Allowing those thoughts to potentially cloud my judgment would only lead to me doing something that I didn't want to do. My mind was made up. Onyx was my past, and I was now looking forward to my future.

Two Months Later

Brittysh

Lost in my thoughts, the abrupt chiming of my phone startled me. Quickly, I grabbed it from my desk to see who was calling me. My heart was beating erratically as I silently prayed it was the one person I desperately wanted to hear from at this very moment. I had been waiting for a while now, but any hope that I had quickly shattered once I noticed X'Zavier's name strolling across the screen. Disappointed, I suddenly let out an exhausting sigh. Instead of answering his call, I opted to ignore it. Right now, I felt like I was a little too anxious to carry on a conversation with him, so I decided it would be best if I sent him a text instead. I waited for a moment. I didn't want him to feel like I was purposely ignoring his calls, even though I actually was. Hurting his feelings was the last thing I really wanted to do. I had to admit that he seemed to be a really nice guy, but I already knew that he wasn't the right one for me. No matter how hard I tried to consider it, he just didn't intrigue me enough to erase what I'd shared with Onyx for so long. There were certain aspects that I required in a man, and X'Zavier just didn't do it for me, even as good-looking as he was. He was a little too predictable for me, and I didn't like that. I needed someone more exciting, and there was nothing about him that excited me in any way.

Me: Hi X'Zavier. Sorry I missed your call. I've been extremely busy all morning. I'll call you back when I go to lunch.

X'Zavier: I understand. I'll be waiting to hear from you. Maybe we can finally make plans to go to dinner?

My eyes rolled once I read his response. Instead of responding to his request, I just ignored it entirely. I'd refused his constant attempts to take me on a date since we first met almost two weeks ago, but he still hadn't gotten the hint. X'Zavier seemed to be a very smart man, but commonsense wasn't one of his strong points. When he first introduced himself to me at a conference that I was scheduled to speak at, I thought he was interested in the article that I'd written that was recently published in one of the clinical journals that were being discussed in the conversation I was having with a few other therapists. When the conversation was over, and the group dispersed, I noticed that he was still sitting at the table gazing in my direction. Feeling a little uncomfortable, I stood up to leave. When he stood up as well and followed me, I quickly let him know that I wasn't interested in anything other than a conversation. Still, he didn't give up. He eventually wore me down, and we exchanged numbers. I had no idea that I would regret it this much. He was a little too persistent for me, and it was becoming somewhat difficult for me to ignore his annoying behavior.

Daily, if he wasn't calling my phone, he was repetitively sending me text messages. It was becoming more and more aggravating as I struggled not to have a miniature breakdown from not knowing what was going on with Onyx. I had prematurely thought that his unforeseen rejection of my love and his sudden disappearance would alleviate any of the apprehension I may have felt about ending our friendship, but that hadn't been the case. Trying to get over him had proven to be extremely harder than I thought it would be. We had soul ties that couldn't be as easily broken. I longed to hear his deep baritone voice, and I couldn't deny it. Not hearing from him was agonizing. It felt like I was only moments away from losing my mind. All I wanted was to see his face just once more, but I wasn't sure if I would ever get the opportunity again.

Onyx's whereabouts constantly monopolized my thoughts; I couldn't even concentrate while I was at work. It was getting the best of me, and I knew my desperate need to make sure he was alright wouldn't go away until I found out something. Even though I had previously decided not to contact Onyx, I'd since realized that wouldn't be possible. I felt like my mind was being held hostage by him; my every thought was continuously preoccupied with the fact that I still hadn't heard a word from him in two months. It was like he'd vanished into thin air. Fear consumed my mind daily as I worried about his safety. Losing his brother had him talking recklessly, and I knew that could be a problem due to the type of lifestyle he lived. I'd actually attempted to reach out to him a couple of times over the last couple of days, but I was only wasting my time. Every time I called his phone, I was sent straight to voicemail. I had tried texting him as well. No matter how many times I sent his ass a text in a day, he ignored them all. I'd even resorted to considering to reach out to Rich, but I decided it was best that I didn't. I wasn't sure if Rich knew about what had transpired between the two of us, so I didn't want to involve him. I was starting to feel like he was purposely ignoring me, and I knew I didn't deserve it even though we'd obviously gone our separate ways.

As I sat in front of my computer tapping a pen against my desk, anger started to radiate from my soul. Every outrageous possibility of what he could be doing seemed to cross my mind. Constantly, I mentally fought against my own self trying to convince myself that he wasn't worth it. He had chosen to walk away from me, and I didn't have the strength to hold on to him any longer. Over and over, I also still wondered if I should've allowed his words to hurt me as much as they did. Reality quickly reminded me that he still hadn't reached out to me to confess his faults, so he must've meant every word. While I was still somewhat pining over him, he was probably somewhere doing whatever he wanted to do at this point. I knew that allowing his shenanigans to get the best of me would eventually drive me insane, but I couldn't control how I felt. He was still somehow controlling my emotions, and I didn't know what to do about it. I fought hard to leave him in the past, but it didn't work.

For so long, I had knowingly accepted Onyx's unfair dismissal of my true feelings. In my heart, I truly believed he loved me. I chose to believe that I could change him if I loved him enough, but that wasn't the case. It took me a while to face the fact that I was the one who had allowed him to continuously treat me the way he did. He had been beyond disrespectful for way too long, so I couldn't help but to also wonder if he was just laid up some-where with the next bitch while I sat around in despair. It seemed as if I was the last person on his mind at the moment. I knew that we didn't have any titles for whatever was going on between us, but I didn't deserve this. Here I was desperate for someone who didn't even know how to love me. My mind was all over the place, and I couldn't control it.

We weren't in a relationship, so I couldn't figure out why I was allowing this situation to torture me. It was true that we shared a very special bond, but it must've only mattered to me. For so long, I thought our friendship meant something to him, but it obviously didn't. We'd been there for one another through any and everything since we met. He knew that I wanted more, but it was just something he wasn't ready to give me. Everybody knew that Onyx was the only man in my life, and I wasn't so sure if I was truly ready for that to change now. I wasn't sure if I could go on without him. My heart was extremely conflicted.

Later that day....

As I sat at my desk trying to focus, my mind continued to wonder. No matter how hard I tried to concentrate on the project I was preparing for one of my group counseling sessions coming up soon, I just couldn't focus. All week I'd tried to concentrate on it, but I just wasn't able to. I had promised my colleagues an update on the details we needed to go over before the session by the end of the week, but I didn't have anything to enlighten them with at this point. The document that I was supposed to be typ-ing on was completely blank.

Breaking me from the mental agony that was torturing me as time slowly coursed by, the alert of an incoming text startled me. I quickly snatched my phone from my desk as I prayed within those few moments that it was him. As soon as my eyes scanned the screen, my heart dropped momentarily. Seeing his best friend Rich's name pop up on my screen caused fear to serge through my body. My hands immediately started to quiver as I tapped on the message. Closing my eyes for a moment, I took a deep breath before reading the text.

Rich: Come outside! I need to holla at you.

Me: I'm at work.

Rich: I know where the fuck you at! Bring yo' ass outside, girl.

Me: This better be worth my time.

Rich: Shut up!

Every time I had any interaction with Rich, we treated each other like enemies. I acted as if I couldn't stand him, but I was only a phone call away if he really needed me. Despite how we treated each other, we were like family. Onyx and Rich were closer than any two people could be, and I respected their friendship no matter how much Rich got on my nerves. I trusted him, so I knew that I was about to get some answers regarding Onyx's whereabouts. Despite how confused I felt about the situation between me and Onyx right now, I still wanted to make sure he was safe.

I quickly rushed out of the building to find Rich. As soon as I walked towards the parking lot, the first vehicle I spotted was Onyx's all-black Range Rover parked next to my car. The moment Rich spotted me, he jumped out of the truck and headed my way. As soon as we were close enough to each other, he started talking really fast as if he was panicking. Unsure of how to react, I abruptly stopped in my tracks. I didn't know what to expect from the way he was acting.

"Sis, some fucked up shit happened last night, and I knew you were the only person who could help me wit' this shit!"

"What happened, Rich?"

"Man, he fucked up pretty bad, and all he keeps askin' about is you."

Before I could open my mouth to say another word, he grabbed my hand and practically dragged me to the back of the truck. Afraid of what he was about to reveal to me, I braced myself. I quickly closed my eyes as he pressed the button to open the back part of the truck. Suddenly, the sound of Onyx's voice forced me to open my eyes immediately.

"Brittysh!"

My heart instantly dropped the moment my eyes landed on him, sitting uncomfortably in the back of his truck with his legs propped up. My eyes scanned his entire body from head to toe to make sure he wasn't hurt in any way. When I suddenly noticed that he was holding a small black box in his hand, I froze. I couldn't speak. I was completely in shock. The stare between the two of us lingered for a moment before he finally opened the box to reveal the massive diamond ring that was inside. My mouth instantly dropped open as I stood there in complete silence, unable to move. Unsure of how to feel, I couldn't find the words to say at that very moment. I almost felt like this had to be some sort of mirage or maybe even a dream, but I knew I wasn't asleep.

"So what's up? You wanna make this shit official wit' a nigga or what?"

I wanted to speak, but nothing would come from my mouth. My throat was completely dry, and I almost felt like I would pass out at any moment. My heart was beating out of control as I suddenly found it hard to breathe while I continued to stand there at a loss for words. This whole situation was just so unbelievable.

"Out of all the times I needed you to hush, you pick this moment to be quiet. Say somethin' to a nigga, baby. This silence got me feelin' some type of way."

"Girl, yo' ass better say yes."

The sound of my sister's nagging voice pulled me out of the trance I'd somehow gotten lost in. Seeing Karmyn here at this moment instantly let me know that she must've known something about what was going to happen. She had been practically ignoring me all week, and now I had an inkling that this was the reason for her behavior. It was obvious that she knew what was going on all along; she was in cahoots with these two mischievous fools, and I had every intention to punish her when she least expected it for keeping something like this from me. I didn't know if I should really be upset with her or not for being a part of this, though; after all, she knew how I felt about him more than anyone else. Once she realized I was giving her the evil eye, she rolled her eyes as if it didn't matter to her one way or another. Instead of continuing our unspoken conversation, I focused my attention back on the man with the question. Finally able to speak, I said the first thing that came to mind.

"I can't believe this. Are you serious right now? Are you really here doing this right now?"

"Believe it, baby. A nigga can't live wit' out yo' ass no more."

As I stared deeply into Onyx's eyes, I searched for the sincerity I needed to see from him to believe this was really happening to me. Even though he was here asking me the one question I longed to hear him ask me, I wasn't sure if this moment was real. I had to admit that I was somewhat apprehensive to trust in him enough to know that his heart had led him to do something as profound as this after all of this time. All of this was so sudden, but it was exactly what my heart had longed for. With tears streaming down my face, my voice trembled as I finally asked the question I needed to ask before committing myself to a lifetime with the only man I'd ever loved.

"Why now?"

"Why not now? Shit, I was a fuckin' fool to wait for this damn long."

"Onyx, I..."

"You what? Please don't say some shit I don't wanna hear right now. I need you to believe in this shit we got going on between us for real, ma. A nigga really love yo' ass, and I can't let nobody else get what I know belongs to me."

"This isn't about anyone else. I never loved anyone as much as I love you. I just can't believe you're here doing this now after everything we've been through. A couple of months ago, well, even a few minutes ago, I wasn't even sure if I would ever see you again after the way things were left between us. You pushed me away, and I didn't know what to do."

As my tears continued to flow, he stood up from where he was sitting in the back of the truck. He quickly filled the space that was separating us. When he pulled me close to his chest, I instantly melted in his arms. It finally felt like I was home again. Nothing in this world compared to how this man made me feel when he held me. Our hearts had always been in sync since the first time I heard his heart beating.

"Yeah, I know I fucked up wit' the way I handled you that night. If I could've kicked my own ass, I would have. It took me a minute to see that shit, though. I was in a fucked-up space mentally, and I didn't wanna see that all you wanted to do was be there for a nigga. That shit was hard, ma. You have to understand that I wasn't thinking right."

"But, I... I..."

"Stop stumblin' over yo' words and say what you need to say, bae."

"I just don't understand. I've been calling you and texting you. Not once have I heard back from you. I felt like you were ignoring me on purpose, and that hurt me even more. You just don't know how I've been going crazy worried about you."

"Ma, I apologize for that shit, for real. I just needed to get my shit right and make sure I was ready for this shit right here. After I lost my damn brother, my momma told my ass that I needed to get my shit together before something fucked up happened to me. I'm the last son she got, so I gotta respect what she asked me to do. She had me feelin' like it was time for me to be a better man, especially for you ma. A nigga ain't never had a woman like you to love him. I wasn't used to that shit, so I didn't know how to receive it. I had to figure that shit out for myself real quick, though. When I heard that some nigga named X'Zavier was tryna get at you, that bullshit fucked me up even more. I couldn't see myself losing you, especially not to some lame ass nigga like that."

"It's not what you think. Wait a minute, how do you even know about him?"

"Let's just say a little birdie made sure I found that shit out. I guess that was her way of tellin' a nigga to get his shit together before she hurt me about her sister."

I glanced to my left, where Karmyn was standing, and the child-like grin on her face confirmed everything Onyx said. My sister was funny like that. She was quick to talk a lot of shit when it came to the situation between Onyx and me, but obviously, she believed in us just as much as I did.

"So, are you here because you're afraid of someone else replacing you, or are you trying to say that you really want to be with me now? I need to know the truth. It doesn't mean anything if all of this is just about another man trying to get my attention."

"Nah, this ain't got shit to do wit' his bitch ass. Hearin' about that muthafucka just opened my damn eyes right on time. Trust me, baby, I wouldn't be here doin' this shit if I didn't mean it. A nigga ain't tryna be out here buyin' rings and shit if I ain't for real. You already know that shit."

"I need to know that you really want this. Onyx, you don't even realize how much I do love you, so this isn't a game to me."

"Listen, I know I ain't perfect, but I know I love yo' ass more than I love my damn self."

"Oh my gosh! Britt, you doin' too much, sis. You know you love this nigga funky, dirty-ass drawers, and you ain't tryna be with nobody else. Can you please put this nigga out of his misery and tell his ass yes? It's hot as hell out here too, and the glue holding down my lace frontal is starting to melt."

"Shut the fuck up! Don't nobody out here wanna hear about yo' damn raggedy-ass wig. You can't rush this shit! My dawg got some shit to explain to this woman before she agrees to marry his ass. Calm the fuck down wit' all that extra shit!"

"Damn nigga! Who fuckin' side you own? You supposed to be my damn brother."

"Hell yeah, Onyx! Tell that nigga to shut the fuck up. He just mad that nobody wants his sorry ass but them ol' tired, dusty ass hoes he keeps fuckin' wit' in the projects."

"You do! That's why you talkin' shit now. Maybe if you get yo' shit together, a nigga might propose to yo' tired ass one day."

"Whateva!"

"Will you both hush! I just need to make sure Onyx really wants to be with me for real this time. We've never actually been in a relationship, so this isn't something I was expecting."

"But the question is do you love him enough to spend the rest of your life with him. Brittysh, you know that you love Onyx. We all know that you do. It's very obvious. As long as you've been my sister, I've never seen you love someone so much. Even though you two never made it official, you actually were in a relationship of some sort. You two have always been there for one another through thick and thin. Trust your feelings, sister. I wouldn't be here if I didn't believe that he really loves you too. Follow your heart."

After listening to my sister tell me how she really felt about the situation between Onyx and me, some of the anxiety I felt disappeared. For some reason, I needed her to see what I could've been blinded by because of my desire to be with him. With her encouragement, it made it easier for me to look into Onyx's eyes and sincerely answer his question. When he firmly held my hands in his, I watched him intently as he knelt down on one knee. As my heart began to flutter at a rapid pace, I prepared myself to answer his question without any apprehension this time.

"So, I hope you ready to answer a nigga this time?"

"I am. I promise."

"Okay. Brittysh, will you marry me, baby? All I want is forever wit' you, ma."

"Yes! Yes, baby, I will marry you."

He jumped up from the position he was knelt in and wrapped his arms around me. When he suddenly picked me up from where I stood, I cried tears of joy as my sister screamed at the top of her lungs. Even Rich had a huge smile on his face as Onyx held me close in his arms. It was the best moment of my life, and I couldn't wait to officially become his wife.

The End

Because you left, my world came to an end...
Then you came back again, now I know...
There is no way that I can go on without you...
I can't go on without you...

~Shirley Murdock~

Other Titles Available By Serica Rena'

I Love You, But We Can't Keep Doing This
(Three-Part Complete Series)

Thought I Was Sleepin' Next To My Superman
(Three-Part Complete Series)

Baby Be Mine
(Finale Coming Soon)

You, Me And Him ~ Novella Series
(Part Two Coming Soon)

Dreaming Of You
(Finale Coming Soon)

Christmas Just Ain't Christmas ~ Novella

Come Through ~ Erotica Novella

More Coming Soon....